JOHNNY'S IN THE BASEMENT

LOUIS SACHAR lives in San Francisco, California, where he writes, practices law, plays chess and rugby, and, like Johnny, occasionally talks to the moon.

JOHNNY'S IN THE BASEMENT

BASEMENT

Louis Sachar

AN AVON CAMELOT BOOK

dedicated to Kevin Lally

6th grade reading level has been determined by using the Fry Readability Scale.

AVON BOOKS, INC.
1350 Avenue of the Americas
New York, New York 10019

Copyright © 1981 by Louis Sachar
Published by arrangement with the author
Visit our website at www.AvonBooks.com
Library of Congress Catalog Card Number: 81-65064
ISBN: 0-380-83451-0

First Avon Camelot Printing: May 1983
First Avon Flare Printing: October 1981

CAMELOT TRADEMARK REG. U.S. PAT. OFF. AND IN OTHER COUNTRIES, MARCA REGISTRADA, HECHO EN U.S.A.

Printed in the U.S.A.

OPM 10

Look out, Kid.

JOHNNY'S IN THE BASEMENT

CHAPTER 1

A Little Kid

When Johnny was nine he received a letter from the President of the United States. It read:

Dear Johnny,
    I heard about your bottle cap collection. I'm glad to be able to do my share.

Yours truly,
The President

Along with the letter came a ginger ale bottle cap. It was bent in the middle from when the President had pried it off with his bottle opener.

Johnny threw the letter away and tossed the bottle cap in with his other ones.

That was about a year and a half ago.

Johnny can remove a bottle cap without bending it.

"John-ny!" called his mother, Carol Laxatayl, from the living room. "Johnny, go to bed. Johnny! Johnny, where *are* you?"

"He's in the basement," said Christene from under the coffee table. Christene was Johnny's little sister who never had to go to bed.

"Princess, do you know where Johnny is?" asked her mother.

Christene bit her finger, then nodded her head.

"John-ny!" called Carol.

It was summertime, just a week after school let out, and the day before Johnny's eleventh birthday.

"Johnny, where are you? It's time for bed! Johnny, I know you can hear me, do you *hear* me?"

Carol worked in a library where she had to keep quiet all day long. When she came home she made up for it by yelling a lot. Mostly, she yelled at Johnny.

"Johnny! Johnny, where are you?"

"He's in the basement," said Christene.

"Princess, do you know where your brother is?" asked Carol.

Christene bit her finger and nodded her head.

"John-ny!"

That last scream woke up Johnny's father, Harry Laxatayl, who had been asleep on the couch. Harry had been out of a job for a while. He was a tall, skinny man with red hair and a red beard. He looked like a red-headed Abe Lincoln.

"What's the matter, Honey?" he asked.

"I can't find Johnny," Carol replied. "It's past his bedtime. John-ny!"

"Princess, where is Johnny?" asked her father.

"He's in the basement, Daddy," said Christene.

"He's in the basement, Honey," repeated Harry.

Mrs. Laxatayl gave her daughter a funny look. "Princess?" she asked. "Why didn't you tell me where he was?"

Christene thought for a second, then replied, "I didn't know you were looking for him." She thought it sounded like a reasonable answer.

Carol threw her hands up in the air, then walked into the hall closet. On the floor there was a trapdoor. She raised it and hollered down into the basement, "Johnny, it's time for bed!"

There was no answer.

10

"Johnny, are you down there?" she called. "Johnny!"

"Did you call me, Mommy?" came the voice from down below.

"Yes I called you!" answered his mother. "I've been calling you for the last ten minutes! It's after ten o'clock!"

"Okay, okay," said Johnny. "You don't have to shout."

He was ten years old and his bedtime was ten o'clock. Tomorrow was his birthday and his bedtime would be changed to ten-thirty, but today he still had to go to bed at ten o'clock. He stepped up from the basement and out of the closet.

His mother smiled when she saw Johnny and Johnny kissed her good night. His father patted him on the back. "Go to sleep, Son. You've got a big day ahead of you."

Johnny walked down the hall toward his room.

"Good night, Johnny," called Christene.

"Night, Christene," said Johnny.

Johnny looked like a dog. Not that he was ugly. No, he was, as they say, "a handsome dog." Besides, dogs aren't ugly. And not all dogs look alike. A Saint Bernard looks nothing like a poodle. But Johnny didn't look like either of those dogs. He looked just like a dog that happened to live only a few blocks away, a mutt by the name of Popover.

Popover had white, silky fur with black around his eyes, and a very curly tail.

Johnny didn't have a tail. Nor did he have white, silky fur with black around his eyes. But he looked like Popover just the same. They had the same expression on their faces.

CHAPTER 2

Some Birthday Presents

Johnny awoke and he wasn't a little kid anymore. He was eleven years old. He looked in the mirror. He still looked the same as he did when he was ten (like a dog). He walked into the kitchen and poured himself a bowl of cereal.

Christene set down her trumpet. "Good morning, Johnny," she said. Christene liked blowing on the trumpet. It gave her something to do while the rest of the family slept.

"Mornin' Christene," said Johnny. "Today is my birthday."

Christene gave Johnny a funny look. "I thought it was last year?"

For his birthday, Johnny would get a nickel raise in his allowance. His bedtime would be changed to ten-thirty. And he'd have a party.

But it wouldn't be much of a party. Johnny had only invited one friend, Donald Duckerman, a kid who lived up the street. All of his other friends were just school friends. His aunts and uncles were coming. He thought that was okay. They would bring him presents, but then he'd have to kiss his aunts.

There are some families where kids even have to

12

kiss their sisters. Johnny was glad his family wasn't like that. It was bad enough having to kiss his aunts.

The party began at a little after two o'clock. He, Donald, and Christene sat on the floor of the living room and took turns playing tic-tac-toe while the adults sat around and drank liquor. Aunt Mary smoked. Johnny hated cigarette smoke. No matter where he sat, the smoke always seemed to go right in his face.

Donald Duckerman was Johnny's best friend, but he wasn't having too much fun because he hated being around adults.

They tied every game of tic-tac-toe. They knew all the secrets.

Donald thought that maybe he ought to go home and clean his room.

Somebody turned out the lights and Mrs. Laxatayl brought out a cake with eleven candles. Everyone sang, "Happy Birthday to You," as Christene tried to play along on her trumpet. Donald sang the same tune but different words.

> Happy birthday to you,
> You smell like your shoes,
> You're dumb and you're ugly,
> We're all glad we're not you.

Johnny made a wish and blew out the candles, ten of them. He was out of air and one still burned.

It was the first time since he was two that he hadn't blown them all out. "I just didn't take a big enough breath," he explained, then blew out the last one.

"Hah! Just wait until you try blowing out fifty-eight," said Uncle Joe who was fifty-eight years old. "I haven't blown out all of my candles since I was ten. Haven't had a wish come true for forty-eight years."

"My wishes almost always come true," said Johnny.

"Not anymore they won't," said Uncle Joe. "You're not a little kid anymore."

Aunt Mary puffed on her cigarette. The smoke went in Johnny's face.

"Hey! What do you say you open your presents," said his mother.

Johnny liked that idea. He opened Uncle Joe's present first. His mouth dropped open. "A potato, an onion, and a thing of sour cream," he muttered. He showed it to Donald.

"A potato, an onion, and sour cream," said Donald.

"Yep!" said Uncle Joe. "A potato, and an onion, and a half a pint of sour cream!"

"Uh, thanks," said Johnny.

"It's symbolic," said Uncle Joe. "Now that you're not a little kid anymore. The potato stands for a lifetime of health, and the onion for a lifetime of happiness."

"Oh, thanks I guess," said Johnny. "What's the sour cream for?"

"The potato!" laughed Uncle Joe who had been just waiting for that question. "I got you something else, too," he said as he reached into his pocket and handed Johnny a dozen bottle caps.

"Thanks," said Johnny.

Next, he opened his mother's present. Socks and underwear.

"You need new underwear," his mother reminded him.

"I guess," said Johnny.

Aunt Sylvia also gave him socks and underwear. "Your mother told me you needed them."

"Well, you can't have too many pairs of socks," said Uncle Todd, and everyone, except Donald, seemed to agree.

Christene gave him a songbook for the trumpet.

"But I don't know how to play a trumpet," said Johnny.

"Oh. Can I have it?" asked Christene.

He opened Donald's present—three toothbrushes and a tube of toothpaste. "You too?" he said.

Donald shrugged his shoulders. "My mother bought it," he said. "I didn't know."

Johnny got a book about Roman architecture from his father.

Uncle Joe's present turned out to be the best. Aunt Mary's was the worst. She gave him dancing lessons at Leonora's Dance Studio. He could just stick his other presents in the back of his closet, but he'd have to start going to Leonora's Dance Studio every Tuesday.

Donald got up to leave.

"Why don't you hang around and play with my birthday presents," said Johnny.

"Some birthday presents!" said Donald. "You just got junk. Anyway, I feel funny being around all your aunts and uncles."

Johnny sat by himself. Aunt Mary's cigarette smoke swirled in his face.

"What's the matter, Son?" asked his father.

"All I got was junk," said Johnny. "How come I didn't get any toys?"

"You're not a little kid anymore," said his father. "You're too old for toys now."

Everyone went home. Johnny had to kiss all of his aunts. He had hoped that maybe since he was too old for toys he was also too old to have to kiss his aunts, but that wasn't the case.

You never outgrow having to kiss your aunts.

CHAPTER 3

Carry the Garbage Around

The next night Christene crawled under the coffee table, took off her shoes and socks, and counted her toes. They were all there.

"John-ny!" screamed her mother. "Princess, where is Johnny?"

"He's in the basement," said Christene.

"I should have known," said her mother. "He's always in the basement. I wonder what he does with those things."

Christene thought it over. "Maybe he eats them," she suggested.

Mrs. Laxatayl laughed. "I doubt it, Princess," she said. "They probably don't taste very good."

"They do too," said Christene.

Carol gave her daughter a funny look. Then she walked into the hall closet, lifted the hatch, and hollered down below, "Johnny! Johnny, are you down there? *Johnny!* Johnny, it's ten o'clock! Johnny! Johnny, can you *hear* me?"

"Did you say something, Mommy?" asked Johnny.

"Come on up here!" called his mother.

"But I don't have to go to bed until ten-thirty," called Johnny.

"Just *come here!*" called his mother, who didn't want to have to shout at him from across the house. She preferred shouting at him from three feet away.

Johnny stomped up into the hall closet and out into the hall. "It's only ten o'clock," he said. "I don't have to go to bed until ten-thirty. I'm eleven years old."

Carol smiled. "I know how old you are," she assured him. "You don't have to go to bed."

"Well, good," said Johnny.

"You just have to do the dishes," she said.

Johnny cocked his head to one side.

"You have to wash the dishes," his mother repeated.

"Huh?" said Johnny.

"Your bedtime is ten-thirty, but before you go to bed you must wash the dishes."

Johnny still didn't understand. "Why?" he asked.

"Because they're dirty," his mother explained.

"Why do *I* have to wash them?" asked Johnny. *"You're* the one who washes the dishes. It's not me. It's you."

"You're eleven years old now," said his mother. "From now on it will be your job."

That didn't make any sense. He walked over to the sink and turned on the water. "I don't even know how to wash dishes," he complained.

"Try," said his mother. "I bet you can figure it out."

Johnny stuck a dish in the soapy water, washed it, and rinsed it off, but it still didn't make any sense.

"Oh, and when you finish, I want you to take the garbage pails around to the front. The garbage men come tomorrow."

"But that's Daddy's job," said Johnny.

"That will be your job now, too," said his mother.

"Daddy won't mind," added Christene.

Johnny continued washing the dishes. "Boy, what's so great about being able to stay up until ten-thirty?" he thought. "Big deal. All you do is wash dishes."

"Here, you forgot a spoon," said Christene.

"Gee, thanks," muttered Johnny. "Don't ever become eleven, Christene," he said.

"I'll try not to," said Christene.

"Remember to carry the garbage around!" called his mother.

"Yeah, yeah," grumbled Johnny.

By the time he had dried the last dish and had taken the garbage cans around to the front, it was time to go to bed.

His father came into his room. "Do you have any plans this weekend, Johnny?" he asked.

"No," said Johnny, thinking that maybe his father might take him to a baseball game.

"Good," his father replied, "because I want you to sweep the garage."

"Oh, I *do* have plans," said Johnny. "Donald and I were going to do some stuff."

"Fine. First you'll sweep the garage," said his father.

"How come?" asked Johnny. "How come I have to do all this—sweep the garage, carry around the garbage, do the dishes? Why? It's not fair."

"You're getting a fifty-five-cent allowance now," said his father. "You have to earn it."

"But when I was ten I didn't have to do anything," said Johnny. "Now I have to do all this stuff for just a nickel."

"Fifty-five cents is more than a nickel," said his father.

"Just a nickel more than I got before," said Johnny.

"John-ny! Johnny go to bed!" called his mother from the living room.

"Just a nickel," said Johnny.

"Johnny, it's ten-thirty! Time for bed!"

"You're getting something else," said his father, "something more important."

"What's that?" asked Johnny.

"Responsibility," said his father.

"John-ny! Johnny, where are you?"

"Respon-si-bility?" asked Johnny.

"That's right, Son," said his father. He patted Johnny on the head, "Good night," and left the room.

"John-ny!" screamed his mother.

It still didn't make much sense. "Did you call me, Mommy?" he asked.

"Yes. Time to go to bed!"

"I'm in bed," said Johnny.

"Oh," his mother replied. "Sleep well."

Johnny lay in bed. "Re-spon-si-bil-i-ty," he thought. He didn't like the sound of that word.

CHAPTER 4

The Frog and the Princess

Saturday morning, Donald Duckerman kicked a rock as he walked down the street to Johnny's house. Donald always kicked a rock wherever he walked. He even kept a couple of rocks in his pockets in case he happened to be on a street without rocks.

There was a fire hydrant in front of the Laxatayls' home. Donald kicked the rock off the fire hydrant, then along the walkway, up on the front stoop, and onto the welcome mat in front of the door.

He noticed an old shoe box with a green ribbon around it lying on the front stoop. Across the top was written "Johnny Laxatayl."

Donald picked up the box and knocked on the door. "Come in," called Mrs. Laxatayl, which he did.

The Laxatayls were sitting around the kitchen table. Mrs. Laxatayl was reading the newspaper. Mr. Laxatayl was just relaxing. Christene was playing around with her cereal. And Johnny was trying to hurry up and gulp down the last half of his breakfast.

"Hey, Johnny, I got a package for you," said Donald.

"Thanks," said Johnny. "What is it?"

"It's not from me," said Donald. "It was on your front stoop." He set it down in the middle of the kitchen table. "Maybe somebody is giving you a pair of his old shoes."

"Or maybe it's a bomb and will blow up when you open it," said Christene.

Johnny pulled off the ribbon without untying it and opened the box. "It's bottle caps," he announced.

"Bottle caps!" said Christene. "I was hoping it would be a bomb."

"Who's it from?" asked his father.

There was no note. "I don't know," said Johnny. He thought it was great. How wonderful it was to get a present and to not even know who sent it. "I bet there's over a hundred in here!" he said.

"So, how have you been, Donald?" asked Mrs. Laxatayl.

"I don't know. Okay, I guess," said Donald. He hated having to talk to his friends' parents.

"And how's your lovely mother?" asked Mrs. Laxatayl.

"She's okay, too," said Donald.

"I keep meaning to have lunch with her," said Mrs. Laxatayl, "but something always comes up. Either I can't get away or she can't."

"Uh huh," said Donald. "Hey, Johnny, you want to go outside or something?"

Johnny had a mouthful of food.

"Donald?" asked Christene. "If you eat a live frog will you be able to jump higher?"

"No, Christene," Donald replied.

"Have you ever eaten one?" Christene asked.

"Of course not," said Donald.

"Well then, how do you know?" asked Christene.

Donald gave Christene a funny look.

"What do frogs taste like?" Christene asked.

21

"I've never eaten one," said Donald.

"Oh, that's right," said Christene. "What *don't* they taste like?"

Johnny swallowed his food. "I can't play yet," he said. "I have to clean the garage."

"Mommy, I don't like this cereal," said Christene. "Do we have any frogs?"

"Eat your cereal, Princess," said Mrs. Laxatayl.

"That's ridiculous," said Donald. "What do you mean you can't play?"

Johnny looked at his father and said, "I've got responsibility."

"What did you do to get that?" asked Donald.

"You have to earn it," said Mr. Laxatayl. "If Johnny does a real good job on the garage today, then next week he will have more responsibility. He'll have to sweep the garage and mow the lawn. And if he does well again, he'll have to wash the car. So long as he works hard and does a good job, he'll keep getting more and more responsibility."

"And what if he does a bad job?" asked Donald.

"I won't let him do any more work," said Mr. Laxatayl.

Donald looked at Johnny, then at Mr. Laxatayl, then back at Johnny.

Johnny shrugged his shoulders.

Donald didn't know what to think. "Well, I guess I'll see you later," he said.

Johnny walked him to the door.

"I don't think responsibility sounds all that terrific," said Donald.

"I know," said Johnny.

Donald looked at the ground, then back up at Johnny. "Hey, how come your parents always call your sister Princess, but they don't call you Prince?" he asked.

Johnny laughed. "I don't know. I guess Prince sounds like a dog's name."

Donald laughed, then said, "Well, you kind of look like a dog."

Johnny pushed Donald out the door.

Donald felt good to be outside. His rock was waiting for him on the welcome mat. He kicked it down the walkway and out past the fire hydrant. Then he kicked it along, up the street, back home.

CHAPTER 5

A Lousy Cookie

Johnny felt like a cookie. He was supposed to be writing thank-you letters for all of his birthday presents. It had been more than a week since his birthday. But he didn't feel like writing any thank-you letters. He felt like a cookie.

His parents were in the living room.

Johnny walked in and asked, "Mommy, can I have a cookie?"

"I don't know. *Can* you?" asked his father.

Johnny hated that kind of stuff. *"May* I have a cookie?" he asked.

"I can't hear you," sang his father.

Johnny hated that, too. "May I have a cookie, *please?"* he asked.

"That's better," said his father. He was lying faceup on the couch. Carol was sitting in the armchair.

Johnny waited. There was still no word on the cookie. "Mommy, may I please have a cookie!"

Carol Laxatayl sighed.

Johnny waited.

His mother appeared to be giving the matter a lot of thought, much more than it deserved. She seemed distressed. At last she said, "Don't call me that anymore, Johnny."

"What? Call you what?" asked Johnny. "I didn't call you anything. All I want is a cookie."

"Don't call me Mommy anymore," said his mother.

Johnny was dumbstruck. "Aren't you my mommy?" he asked.

"You're too old to call me Mommy," his mother explained.

"But that's who you are!" Johnny insisted. "You're Mommy."

His mother sighed. "No I'm not, not anymore."

"You're eleven years old now," said his father. "You're not a little kid anymore. You shouldn't use that word."

"Doesn't she love me anymore?" asked Johnny.

"Of course I love you, Johnny," said his mother. "But my name is not Mommy."

"Mom-my," called Christene from the other room. "The mail's here."

"Bring it into the living room, Princess," replied her mother.

Johnny felt tears coming to his eyes. "Christene called you Mommy," he whined.

"Christene is only five years old," said his mother.

"But I love you," said Johnny.

"We love you, too," said his father.

Christene appeared with the mail and handed it to her father.

"Well, what do you know, Princess," he said. "There's a letter here for you."

"From whom?" asked Mrs. Laxatayl.

Christene grabbed the letter. "From me!" she said. "Nobody else ever sends me any mail so I sent one to myself."

"But you can't write," said her mother.

"And I can't read either," said Christene. "Daddy undressed the envelope for me." She took her letter outside to play with.

Mr. Laxatayl put the rest of the letters down on the coffee table. Johnny poked through them, looking at the different envelopes addressed to his mother.

"Well, what can I call you?" he asked. "Carol?"

"Certainly not," said his mother.

"Well, how about Mrs. Laxatayl?" he asked.

"I don't think so," said his mother.

"Well, what does Daddy, er, what does *he* call you?" asked Johnny as he pointed to his father.

"What do you call me, Dear?" asked Carol.

"I call you Honey, Honey," answered Harry.

"Okay, I'll call you Honey," said Johnny.

"You will not," said his mother.

"Well then, what can I call you?" Johnny pleaded.

"You may call me Mother," replied his mother.

"Mother," repeated Johnny. "That sounds terrible. I just won't call you anything."

He didn't feel like a cookie anymore.

CHAPTER 6

A Dancing School

Johnny was wearing his good shoes—the ones that were too tight, and stiff, and hurt his feet. "I hate dancing school," he said.

"You haven't even *gone* there yet!" shouted his mother. "You can't hate it until *after* you've been there!"

"Then you can hate it," added his father.

Mrs. Laxatayl gave her husband a dirty look.

Of all his birthday presents, this one was the worst. Every week he'd have to go to Leonora's Dance Studio.

"I'll hate it. I know I'll hate it," said Johnny.

"Will you quit saying that!" yelled his mother. "Just give it a chance. I bet you'll be pleasantly surprised. Think of all the pretty girls that will be there."

"Yech!" said Johnny.

"Give it a fair chance, Son," said his father.

"Okay," said Johnny. "I'll give it a chance, but I'll still hate it." He opened the front door. His feet hurt.

"Have a nice time, Dear," called his mother.

Johnny slammed the door.

"I hope he doesn't hate it," said Carol.

27

"Are you kidding?" answered Harry. "Of course he'll hate it. Wouldn't you?"

Johnny got his bike out of the garage. It was an ugly, fat, homemade, monster bicycle. Johnny adored it. Uncle Joe's father had built it a long time ago for Uncle Joe when he was a boy. It was indestructible. The wheels weren't exactly round but they never went flat because there was no air in them. They were made of solid rubber. It could never win a race, but for cutting across ditches or going off cliffs there was none better. And it even had a name—Zordtch. Uncle Joe's father named it that. People used to name their bicycles.

Johnny rode over the curb and up the street past the Duckermans'.

"Hey, Johnny! Where are you going?" called Donald.

"Nowhere," Johnny answered. "I'm going nowhere."

"Can I come?" called Donald.

But Johnny pedaled away before Donald could find out where he was really going.

Zordtch didn't have any brakes. Johnny smashed into the side of Leonora's Dance Studio to stop. He let Zordtch fall on the sidewalk and walked inside. His shoes were too tight.

Leonora's Dance Studio was just a big room with a row of chairs on either side and a record player in the corner. There was a mess of kids standing around but nobody talked to anybody else. Johnny hated it, and he hated all the other kids, too. He hated anyone who would go to a dancing school.

The other kids felt the same way. They also hated everybody. But there was one kid who hated it more than anyone, even more than Johnny. Her name was Valerie Plum. She stood in the corner and stared at her feet. Her shoes were too tight.

In the center of the room stood a strange-looking woman all dressed in black. She could have been twenty-five or eighty-five yeàrs old. "My name is Leonora," she said. "Welcome to dancing school."

Valerie Plum grumbled. "Just so long as there's no dancing," she thought.

Valerie lived a few blocks away from Johnny. The Plums had a pet dog with white, silky fur, black eyes, and a very curly tail. It was a mutt named Popover.

"Now," said Leonora, "I want everyone to pick a partner and we'll learn our first dance."

Everyone kind of stood around and tried to hide behind each other.

Valerie Plum looked up defiantly, ready to sock anyone who tried to pick her. Then she saw Johnny. She laughed. She couldn't help it. It was his face. It was the funniest thing she'd ever seen. He looked just like her dog! She walked right up to him and asked him to be her partner.

"Aaagh!" gasped Johnny.

That made Valerie laugh more.

"Fine," said Leonora. "We have our first couple. You can demonstrate the first dance to the rest of the class."

"But I don't know how to dance," protested Johnny.

"Yes, I know," said Leonora. "That's why you're here."

"I'm here because of Aunt Mary," thought Johnny. He glared at the girl who had picked him.

Valerie smiled at Johnny. The madder he got, the funnier he looked.

"Put that arm like this and this arm like that," said Leonora.

Johnny had to put his arms around the girl. His feet hurt.

Leonora turned on the record player and called out instructions along with the music. "And one, and two, and step and back and side and back and back and back and toe and step and heel and step . . ." and Johnny tried his best to keep up but he always seemed to be one step behind, ". . . and slide and back and

29

turn and step . . ." and "What am I doing here?" he wondered. Everyone was staring at him. ". . . and toe and heel . . ." and he hated it. It was worse than he even imagined. ". . . and back and turn . . ." and he hated that girl who had picked him.

Valerie was happy. Every time she looked up and saw her dog's face on the boy with whom she was dancing, she just had to laugh. It was like dancing with her dog. Except, Popover was a better dancer.

". . . and side and step and back and step and toe and heel and step and very good." The music stopped. "Thank you," said Leonora. "That was excellent."

"That stunk!" thought Johnny.

"What's your name?" asked Valerie.

"Johnny Laxatayl," said Johnny.

Valerie smiled. "I'm Valerie Plum," she said.

"Who cares," said Johnny.

Valerie had thought she was going to hate dancing school. But who would have thought she was going to meet someone who looked like her dog? She danced every dance with him.

As soon as class ended, Johnny ran out the door.

"Bye, Johnny!" called Valerie.

Johnny picked up Zordtch and rode home as fast as he could go.

The first thing he did when he got home was take off his shoes.

CHAPTER 7

Someone to Talk to

For dinner the Laxatayls had split pea soup, peas and carrots, chicken pot pie (with peas), and for dessert some kind of green Jell-O. Johnny thought it was a good dinner except he didn't like peas.

"How was dance class?" asked his mother.

"It was terrible," replied Johnny. "I hated it."

"That's nice," said his mother, who wasn't paying attention to the conversation. She had had a tough day at work.

Johnny thought about Valerie Plum. He thought she had a pretty name. He hated her but she had a nice name.

After dinner he washed and dried the dishes. He had found it was better to wash them right away rather than wait until ten o'clock. If he waited, the food stuck to the dishes and they were harder to clean.

"I'm going to Donald's," he announced.

His parents were in the living room. "Okay, Dear," called his mother. "Be back by seven-thirty."

"Seven-thirty?" exclaimed Johnny.

"All right, eight o'clock," said his mother.

"Eight o'clock?!" exclaimed Johnny.

"I think he's old enough to stay out until eight-thirty," said Harry.

"Okay, eight-thirty," called his mother.

"Eight-thirty?!" exclaimed Johnny. Actually, he thought eight-thirty was very fair.

"Nine o'clock," said his father, "and not a second later."

"But I don't have to be in bed until ten-thirty," said Johnny. "What do you want me to do, *watch television?"*

"He *has* shown a lot of responsibility lately," said Carol.

"Nine-thirty," said his father.

One more try. "Nine-thirty?!"

"Ten o'clock!!" screamed his mother. *"Now get out of here!"*

Johnny ran outside and up the street to the Duckermans', thinking he had handled it pretty well. Maybe that responsibility stuff wasn't all that bad after all.

Donald had a basketball court in his backyard. He could make a basket from anywhere in the yard, thanks to a certain home court advantage. There was a big tree in the middle of the yard. From anywhere in the yard, Donald could bounce the ball off the tree and into the basket. However, his best shot was from directly behind the tree where he would throw the ball through a special place between the branches. It would land on top of one branch then roll down another and through the hoop without touching the rim.

He and Johnny played basketball until eight o'clock. Donald won every game.

"I've got to go in now," said Donald.

"But it's only eight o'clock," said Johnny.

"I have to be in by eight," said Donald.

"Come on, one more game," said Johnny. "I can stay out until ten."

"I can't," said Donald. "Anyway, it's getting too dark to see the ball." He went inside.

Johnny slowly walked back down the street. "Now what am I going to do until ten o'clock?" Donald was right, it was getting dark. He sat down on the fire hydrant in front of his house. He wanted someone to talk to. He thought about Valerie Plum.

A grey and white cat walked along the curb.

"Here, kitty. Here, kitty, kitty," called Johnny.

The cat ignored him.

Johnny took a step toward it and the cat ran away.

He sat back down on the fire hydrant. He thought about Valerie Plum. He didn't think anything particular about her. He just thought about her.

He got up and started walking to the corner. He just wished he had someone to talk to. He kept thinking about Valerie. He couldn't get her out of his mind. She just stuck there. He saw two people walking toward him, Mr. and Mrs. Warner. He kept his eyes on them as they walked closer. Finally, when they were close enough, he said, "Hi."

"Hi, Johnny," answered Mrs. Warner as she and her husband walked on. Johnny walked to the corner. Then he kept on walking around the block.

It was dark. He wanted someone to talk to. He thought Valerie Plum had a pretty name.

He found a bottle cap on the sidewalk, put it in his pocket, and continued walking.

The Warners passed him again. Evidently they were walking around the block in the opposite direction.

"Hi," said Johnny.

"Hi," they answered.

Johnny returned home and thought that maybe it was ten o'clock. He opened the door and asked.

"Eight-thirty," replied his mother. "You still have plenty of time."

"Good," said Johnny. "Just checking." He sat on

the fire hydrant. He didn't want to go inside at eight-thirty, after fighting to get to stay out until ten.

He wanted someone to talk to and he thought about Valerie Plum. It began to bother him. "Why do I keep thinking about her?" he wondered. He thought about the way she smiled at him when they were dancing.

He looked up at the sky, hoping to see a shooting star or maybe even a UFO. The moon was out, and a few stars.

Johnny stared at the moon. It was getting a little cold. He stretched and yawned while at the same moment a dog howled at the moon.

"What's wrong? asked the moon.

Johnny cocked his head.

"Look, I don't have all night," said the moon. "I've got to be in China in the morning."

"Are you talking to me?" asked Johnny.

"I ain't talkin' to the man in the moon," laughed the moon. "Look, Kid, don't you have anything better to do?"

Johnny shrugged. "No, I don't. I have to stay out here because I got in a fight with my parents."

"Kicked you out, huh?" said the moon.

"No," said Johnny. "Nothing like that. They wanted me to come in at seven-thirty and I argued with them so they let me stay out until ten."

"And now you're stuck with it," said the moon, "with nothing to do."

"Yep," said Johnny.

"Well, just don't go in before ten o'clock," said the moon, "or else you'll never get to do anything again. Your parents will say,"—the moon affected a high and whiny voice—" 'We know what's best for you. Remember what happened the night you wanted to stay out until ten.' "

Johnny was getting cold. "You think it's almost ten o'clock?" he asked.

"Not even nine," said the moon.

Johnny sat and shivered. At least he had someone to talk to.

"How old are you, about nine, ten?" asked the moon.

"I'm eleven," said Johnny.

"So you're not a little kid anymore," said the moon.

"That's what everyone says," said Johnny.

"You want some advice?" asked the moon.

"I guess," said Johnny.

"Don't fall in love," warned the moon.

Johnny laughed. "I'm not going to fall in love," he said.

"Sure, go ahead and laugh," said the moon. "It's real funny. Ha ha ha! That's what everybody thinks. But then, before you know it, it will sneak up on you and get you."

"I'm not going to fall in love," said Johnny.

"Just look out, Kid," said the moon.

Johnny shivered. "Is it ten o'clock yet?" he asked.

"Five after nine," said the moon.

Johnny sat and waited. He looked at the moon and thought about Valerie Plum. "Hey, how come you're talking to me all of a sudden?" he asked.

"I talk to lonely dogs," said the moon. "You look like a dog."

"Gee, thanks," said Johnny.

"And you howled," the moon added.

"I didn't howl," said Johnny. "I yawned, I think, but I didn't howl. I've never howled."

"Someone howled," said the moon.

"Well, it wasn't me," said Johnny.

"Oh," said the moon, "oh."

Johnny sat and waited. "Now what time is it?"

"A quarter after nine," said the moon.

He waited for what seemed like hours until finally the moon told him it was ten o'clock. "But don't go in yet. You have to make it seem as if you were having a good time."

Johnny waited a bit longer.

35

"And remember what I said about falling in love," warned the moon.

"Okay, sure," said Johnny.

"Johnny! Johnny, time to come in!" called his mother.

"Wait," said the moon. "Make her call you again."

"John-ny! It's ten o'clock!"

"Already?!" exclaimed Johnny as he went inside.

CHAPTER 8

Some Bottle Caps

Donald Duckerman was playing with dirt out in his front yard when Valerie Plum walked by.

"Excuse me," she said. "Do you know where Johnny Laxatayl lives?"

Donald pointed down the street. "It's the one with the fire hydrant in front."

"Thank you," said Valerie.

"You know Johnny?" asked Donald.

"Uh huh," said Valerie as she put her hands in her pockets.

"What are you, his cousin or something?" asked Donald.

"No," said Valerie. "We're in dance class together."

"Dance class!" exclaimed Donald. "Johnny goes to dance class! Oh man, oh man."

"What's wrong with dance class?" asked Valerie. Donald laughed.

"What's wrong with dance class?" Valerie demanded.

"If you don't know, I'm not going to tell you," said Donald.

"It's better than playing with dirt," said Valerie.

"What's wrong with playing with dirt?" asked Donald.

Valerie turned and walked down the street.

"Hey! What's wrong with playing with dirt?" called Donald.

Valerie smiled to herself and kept walking.

"It's better than dance class!" shouted Donald.

Valerie walked up to the house with the fire hydrant in front and knocked on the door.

Johnny was in the basement. His mother was working at the library. His father was relaxing in the living room. Christene answered the door.

"Is Johnny here?" asked Valerie.

"Who?" asked Christene.

"Johnny Lax-a-tayl," said Valerie.

Christene shook her head.

"He's not here?" asked Valerie.

"Nope," said Christene.

"Does he live here? Is this the right house?"

Christene shook her head.

"Do you know where he lives?" asked Valerie.

"Never heard of him," said Christene.

"Oh," said Valerie. She looked up at the number next to the door, the same address she had found in the phone book earlier that morning. "Sorry to bother you."

At that moment Harry Laxatayl came to the door. "Yes, may I help you?" he asked.

"I'm looking for the Laxatayl residence," said Valerie.

"This is the place," said Mr. Laxatayl.

"Is Johnny here?" asked Valerie.

"He's in the basement," said Harry. "Through the hall closet and down the hatch."

Valerie stepped inside. She gave Christene a funny look. Then she walked into the hall closet.

"Does Johnny Laxatayl live here, Daddy?" asked Christene.

"Yes, Princess. He's your brother," replied her father.

"Oh, him!" said Christene.

Valerie lifted the heavy hatch and stepped down the twisting, creaking staircase. The stairs wound around so much that she couldn't see the rest of the basement until she was on the bottom stair. And when she reached the bottom stair, she couldn't believe what she saw.

Bottle caps.

The basement was loaded with bottle caps, piles and piles of them. Valerie couldn't even see the floor. There was a layer of bottle caps covering the entire floor which she figured was at least ten inches high. In places, there were piles three or four feet high. Johnny was sitting on a pile in the center that was over four feet high. "Oh, it's you," he said.

"Hi, Johnny," said Valerie. She looked around in amazement.

"What do you want?" asked Johnny.

Valerie smiled at the boy who looked like her dog. She stepped gingerly across the bottle caps and sat down about ten feet away from Johnny.

"What are you doing here?" Johnny demanded.

Valerie picked up a handful of bottle caps and slowly dropped them one at a time.

Johnny sighed.

"What a terrific collection of bottle caps!" said Valerie.

"You like it?" asked Johnny.

"I think it's wonderful," said Valerie.

"You do?" asked Johnny.

"Oh, yes! And you have so many different kinds, too: Pepsi, Dr. Pepper, Mountain Dew. What's this one?" she asked and held up a bottle cap.

"Let me see," said Johnny.

Valerie stepped across the bottle caps and sat on the pile next to Johnny. She handed him the bottle cap.

Johnny looked at it. "Orange Crush," he said.

"That's so neat," said Valerie. "You can tell what they are just by looking at them."

Johnny beamed. "Aw, it's nothing," he said. "Besides, it's printed right across the top."

"Maybe," said Valerie. "But you're an expert."

"I guess so," said Johnny. "I've been collecting them all my life." He picked up a bottle cap that had "Tab" printed across the top, studied it carefully, and said, "This one's a Tab."

"Boy, that's great," said Valerie.

Johnny beamed.

Valerie picked up a bottle cap. She snapped her fingers and sent it sailing across the room.

"Wow, how'd you do that?" asked Johnny.

"Oh, it's easy," said Valerie, a little surprised that Johnny didn't know how to flick a bottle cap. "Here, just hold your hand like you're going to snap your fingers, then place a bottle cap between your first and third fingers and *snap*." She sent another bottle cap flying across the room.

Johnny tried. When he snapped his fingers, the bottle cap just fell straight down.

"Don't move your hand," said Valerie. "It's all in the fingers."

Johnny tried again, but the same thing happened.

"Don't move your hand," said Valerie.

"I didn't move my hand," said Johnny.

He tried again.

"You moved your hand," said Valerie.

"I did not," said Johnny.

She thought it was funny, like Popover trying to snap his paws.

They played in the basement most of the afternoon, until Valerie had to leave.

"I bet you have over a million," she said. "Where'd you get them all?"

"I don't know," said Johnny.

"What do you mean, you don't know?" said Valerie.

"I don't know," said Johnny. "I've been collecting them a long time. And people just give them to me, people I don't even know."

"Why do they give them to you?" asked Valerie.

"I don't know," said Johnny. "I guess they really just like collecting bottle caps, only they feel stupid so they give them to me. It's fun to collect them. They say they just do it for me, but they don't even know who I am. They just do it because it's fun and then they give them to me so that they don't feel silly."

"Once you have the greatest bottle cap collection in the world it's no longer silly," said Valerie.

"Nobody ever comes over without bringing some bottle caps," said Johnny.

"I will too," said Valerie. "I'll bring a whole bunch."

"You're gonna come over again?" asked Johnny.

"I'll be back," said Valerie.

Johnny followed her up the stairs and to the door. He watched her walk up the street. "I'll see you at dance class!" he called after her, then quickly covered his mouth in horror, unable to believe what he had just shouted for the whole world to hear.

CHAPTER 9

Whowhatt??

Johnny sat with his father in the living room. His mother was still at work. Christene was somewhere.

"Your mother is a wonderful person," stated his father.

Johnny shrugged his shoulders. "She's my mother," he mumbled.

"I know," said his father. He smiled. "She's the one who yells at you all the time."

Johnny laughed. He didn't think his father noticed that she yelled a lot.

"But what do you think about her?" asked his father.

"I don't think about her," said Johnny.

"She's only been your mother for eleven years," said his father. "That's less then a third of her life. For most of her life she didn't know you, or me for that matter."

"I think she's always know us," said Christene from under the coffee table, "even before Johnny and I were born."

"I guess so, Princess," said her father. "Deep down I guess we've both always known both of you. I just want you to realize that besides being your mother, she's also a wonderful person."

"I'm going to Donald's now," said Johnny, feeling uneasy. He got up and walked out the door and up to the Duckermans'. He didn't like thinking about his mother as a real person, just like everybody else. It scared him.

"Did you tell Mommy that she's wonderful, Daddy?" asked Christene.

Harry thought a minute. "No, Princess, I guess I haven't," he said. "Do you think I should?"

Christene nodded her head and said, "I don't know."

Johnny and Donald sat on the curb in front of Donald's house. A neighbor was washing his car. Johnny watched a popsicle stick as it drifted through the gutter water.

"So how was dance class?" asked Donald.

"Whowhatt??" stammered Johnny. He felt as if he'd just been slapped across the face with a dead fish.

"Are you a good dancer?" teased Donald.

"What are you talking about?" asked Johnny.

"You've been going to dancing school," said Donald.

"I have not!" Johnny insisted.

"Have too," said Donald.

"Liar!" said Johnny.

"You and that girl," said Donald. "You've been going to dancing school together. I hear you are a *marvelous* dancer."

"What girl?" Johnny asked.

"The girl that came over to your house the other day," said Donald. "That girl."

"No girl came over to my house," said Johnny.

"I bet you just danced all day with her," said Donald.

"We never danced," declared Johnny, glad to be able to tell the truth for once.

"Ah hah!" exclaimed Donald. "You admitted it. You said 'we.' That proves you were with her."

"No it doesn't," said Johnny, trying to figure a way out. "*We* never danced because she wasn't there. She was at her house and I was at mine."

"Who's she?" asked Donald.

"Who?" asked Johnny.

"The girl who wasn't there," said Donald. "Who is she?"

"I don't know," said Johnny. "I never met her before."

"Ah hah!" exclaimed Donald, thinking he had finally trapped Johnny. "If you don't know who she is, then how do you know you've never met her?"

"Because," replied Johnny, "if I met her then I'd know who she is."

Donald tried to figure out if that made sense. He rubbed the back of his neck and sighed. "Alright," he said. "What *did* you do last Thursday?"

"Nothing," answered Johnny. "I just sat in the basement with my bottle caps."

"You and your stupid bottle caps," muttered Donald.

"It's not stupid," said Johnny. "It's the best bottle cap collection in the world."

"So what?" said Donald. "It's still stupid."

"Valerie likes it," said Johnny. "Oops!"

"Ah hah!" exclaimed Donald. "She was there."

"Was not!" said Johnny.

"Then who's Valerie?" asked Donald.

"Valerie's my sister," said Johnny.

"Your sister's name is Christene," said Donald.

"Valerie!" Johnny insisted.

"Christene," maintained Donald.

"I ought to know her name," said Johnny. "She's my sister."

"That doesn't matter," said Donald. "Her name is Christene." He jumped up from the curb and ran down the street.

Johnny raced after him and passed him as he reached the fire hydrant. Johnny ran up the front walk, flung open the door, and announced, "My sister's name is Valerie."

Harry Laxatayl walked into the hall.

"My sister's name is Valerie," Johnny repeated. "It's Valerie."

Donald was right behind him. "Her name is Christene, isn't it, Mr. Laxatayl?"

Harry smiled at the two boys and said, "I always thought it was Princess."

"My name is Christene," declared Christene from under the coffee table.

"See," said Donald.

"Well, what does she know?" said Johnny. "She's only five years old." He sighed. But then he got an idea. He smiled. "So?" he said. "Her name is Christene, so what?"

Donald became confused. He knew her name was Christene. What did that have to do with anything? It had always been Christene. Somehow that was supposed to prove that Johnny went to dance class. How? He stepped outside, took a rock out of his pocket, and dropped it on the concrete. He slowly kicked it on up the street and tried to figure it out.

But he knew one thing. He didn't like Valerie, whoever she was.

CHAPTER 10

Some Advice

Johnny sat out in front of his house. A dog howled at the moon. The night air felt good. Johnny waited for the dog to finish. He was not one to interrupt another's conversation.

The moon eased between the clouds. The dog was now quiet.

"Duckerman found out about dancing school," said Johnny.

"Duckerman's a cluck," said the moon.

"He found out about Valerie, too," said Johnny.

"Tell Duckerman to— Wait a second. Who is this Duckerman character?" asked the moon.

"He's my best friend," said Johnny.

"Friends, hah!" scoffed the moon. "Punch him in the nose. You don't want any friends. You just have to be nice to them. You want a friend? You really want a friend? Get a dog."

"My mother won't let me have a dog," said Johnny.

"So what's this dancing school nonsense? And who, pray tell, is Valerie?" asked the moon.

"Her name is Valerie Plum," said Johnny. "I have to go to dance class every Tuesday because my Aunt Mary gave me dancing lessons for my birthday."

"Some birthday present!" scoffed the moon.

"You think that's bad," said Johnny, "you should see what else I got."

"Tell me about this Valerie Plum," said the moon.

"She's a girl I met at dancing school," said Johnny. "She asked me to dance and then she came over Thursday to look at my bottle cap collection. Somehow Duckerman found out about it."

"Hey, I hear that's quite a bottle cap collection you have there, maybe the best in the world."

"Thanks," said Johnny. "I've been collecting them all—"

"I don't like the sound of this Valerie Plum," said the moon. "Why'd she pick you?"

"I don't know," said Johnny. "I never thought of that."

"Is she pretty?" asked the moon.

Johnny smiled. "I guess she is," he said.

"Is she nice?" asked the moon.

"Very nice," said Johnny.

"Is she smart?" asked the moon.

"I don't know," laughed Johnny. "I didn't give her a test."

"Are you in love with her?" asked the moon.

"No!" exclaimed Johnny.

"Good, then it's not too late," said the moon. "Don't have anything to do with her anymore. Don't even talk to her. And especially, don't dance with her! If she asks you to dance again, punch her in the nose."

"I sort of like dancing with her," said Johnny. "I mean, if I have to dance with somebody, it might as well be her. I won't fall in love with her or anything."

"Why take chances?" asked the moon.

"Just one dance," said Johnny.

"Just one dance," repeated the moon. "How many times have I heard that before? Then it's 'one more dance.' And then another one after that, and the next

47

thing you know you're taking her for long walks in the park."

"One dance," said Johnny.

"You're playing with fire, Johnny," said the moon. "It's like smoking cigarettes. At first all you want to do is try them. They taste terrible and make you cough. But then you smoke another one, then another, then the next thing you know you're hooked on the disgusting things."

"Okay," sighed Johnny. "I won't dance with her."

"Don't do me any favors," said the moon. "It's for your own good. Well, I've got to go now. I have to be in China by the morning."

"Bye," said Johnny. "And thanks."

"Wait. One more thing," said the moon. "Don't ever say thank you."

"Sorry," said Johnny.

"Not that word either," said the moon.

"Oh, sorry," said Johnny.

"You said it again!" said the moon.

"Sorry," said Johnny. "Oops, sorry, I didn't mean to say that. Oh, I said it again, didn't I? Sorry. Ooops, sorry. Oops, sorry. Ooops, sorry oops, sorry ooops, well you know what I mean."

The moon drifted behind a cloud.

CHAPTER 11

Just One Dance

Tuesday, Johnny rode Zordtch to Leonora's Dance Studio and if Valerie Plum asked him to dance he was going to punch her in the nose.

Zordtch smashed into the side of the building harder than Johnny had expected. He got off, a little dazed, and stumbled inside.

Valerie was waving at him. "Hi, Johnny!" she called.

Johnny smiled. He didn't mean to. It just slipped out.

Valerie hurried up to him. "I brought you some bottle caps for your collection," she said.

"Oh, thanks," muttered Johnny.

Valerie handed him four bottle caps and Johnny put them in his pocket.

"Hold on," said Valerie. "I have more." She pulled six more bottle caps out of her pocket and gave them to him.

Johnny tried not to smile.

"Wait a second, I have a few more," said Valerie. She pulled a dozen more bottle caps from her pocket. "And more," she laughed, as she pulled a handful of bottle caps from another pocket.

Johnny grinned and stuffed them in his pockets.

Valerie couldn't stop laughing. "I've still got more," she said as she emptied another one of her pockets.

Johnny was quickly running out of room for them all. Valerie just kept on handing him more and more bottle caps. "W-wait," he laughed, then began putting them in his shoes and socks.

"One more," said Valerie.

"I've got no more room for it," laughed Johnny. "I'm full."

Valerie placed it behind his ear.

The music started, Johnny put his arms around Valerie and they danced. Johnny felt as if he were dancing across the clouds. He didn't think he knew how to dance, but it was easy dancing with Valerie. She was as light as a feather.

The other kids just sort of fumbled and grumbled around. Leonora paired them up and made them dance, but they weren't very good dancers. Mostly, they just kicked each other. And they all thought that Johnny and Valerie were the biggest dopes they'd ever seen.

Johnny looked at Valerie. Her eyes were like rainbows. He stared deep in her eyes and got lost. He saw snowflakes, and meadows, and forests, and flowers, and waterfalls.

Valerie looked into Johnny's soft, warm, Popover eyes and melted.

Suddenly she realized the music had stopped. She looked around and saw all of the other kids leaving. The class was over. The time had flown by. Johnny was still dancing.

"Johnny!" she whispered sharply, "Johnny. It's time to go. The music's over."

Johnny looked around in confusion. "What music? I don't hear any music."

"Time to go home," said Valerie.

Johnny shook his head. He walked outside, picked up Zordtch, and pedaled home, still lost in another world. He pedaled faster and faster, harder and harder, when *bammm!* He crashed into the fire hydrant in front of his house, flew off the bicycle, did a complete somersault in midair, and landed flat on his back on the front lawn.

He came to his senses. He looked around. His clothes were torn. His elbow was bleeding and his leg hurt. His ankle was twisted. But, at least, it had finally knocked some sense into him.

"Ohhhh," he moaned.

There were bottle caps all over the yard.

CHAPTER 12

Best Friends

Donald Duckerman rarely had both shoes tied at the same time. It didn't bother him at all. He thought it was okay to be sloppy. He was still only ten years old, just a little kid. As soon as he turned eleven he'd have to be clean and neat for the rest of his life, so he might as well be sloppy while he was still ten.

His hair was never combed. His fingernails were always dirty, except on Sundays when he cleaned them. No one had ever seen his shirttail tucked in. And occasionally someone would have to whisper for him to zip up his fly.

He kicked a rock down the street to Johnny's. He kicked it up onto the curb next to the fire hydrant. Then, in one kick, he sent it an inch away from the Laxatayls' door, without ever touching the door. He may have been the best rock kicker in town.

He knocked on the door. He never rang doorbells, always knocked.

Mr. Laxatayl opened the door. "Johnny's in the basement," he said.

Donald stepped inside. Mr. Laxatayl rubbed the top of Donald's head. Adults were always rubbing the top of Donald's head. What's the point of combing your hair if adults are always rubbing the top of your head?

Christene watched from under the coffee table.

Donald stepped into the hall closet and then down to the greatest bottle cap collection in the world.

"I figured it out," he said. "Your sister's name is Christene. You go to dancing school with a girl named Valerie."

Johnny punched him in the nose.

Donald stumbled back. Then he stepped up and hit Johnny in the ear.

Johnny fell over a pile of bottle caps and Donald jumped on top of him. He put his hand on Johnny's chin and pushed his head under the bottle caps.

Johnny grabbed Donald's elbow and pulled his arm away. He pulled his head up from under the bottle caps and rolled over on top of Donald. "I don't go to dancing school!" he declared.

Donald rolled over on top of Johnny. "You can go there if you want," he said. "I don't care."

Johnny tried to push Donald off of him. "But I don't," he insisted.

"If you want to be a ballerina, that's fine with me," said Donald.

Johnny groaned and threw Donald off of him, sending him headfirst into a pile of bottle caps.

"Gahck!" groaned Donald. "I bet you look real cute in pink leotards."

Johnny jammed his knee into Donald's stomach.

"Oomph!" gasped Donald. "Did you learn that at dancing school?"

Johnny pushed Donald's face into the bottle caps. Donald tried to kick him, but Johnny grabbed his leg and dragged him across the room.

Donald spit a bottle cap out of his mouth. "Is this the tango?" he groaned.

Johnny jumped on him. Donald spun around and got Johnny in a headlock. Johnny thrashed his arms wildly and struggled to get free, but Donald had a tight grip. Then Johnny realized that the headlock didn't hurt. He couldn't get loose but it didn't hurt. So he waited a minute and saved his strength, then suddenly lurched free.

The two boys fell in opposite directions. They scrambled toward each other and rolled and tumbled from one end of the basement to the other, then back again.

They struggled to their feet, glared at each other, then laughed and sat down across from each other.

"Whew," said Donald.

"Some fight, huh?" asked Johnny.

"It was great, wasn't it?" asked Donald.

"Sure beats dancing," said Johnny.

They both laughed.

"I've got to get going," said Donald. "We're going to my grandmother's, and I promised my mom I wouldn't get my clothes dirty."

Johnny was exhausted. He lay back on the bottle caps and watched his best friend walk up the stairs to the hall closet.

Donald stepped out into the hall. His hair was a mess. His shirt was untucked. His face was dirty. His pants were torn. His shoes were untied. He looked just the way he had when he arrived.

"Going already, Donald?" asked Mr. Laxatayl.

"Uh huh," said Donald. "I have to go to my grandmother's house."

"What did you boys do?" asked Mr. Laxatayl.

"Nothing," said Donald. "Just danced."

Mr. Laxatyl rubbed the top of Donald's head.

"Good-bye, Donald," called Christene from under the coffee table.

"Bye, Valerie," said Donald.

He kicked his rock back home.

CHAPTER 13

Pig Slop

Above, the stars twinkled. They were over a million miles away, yet still they twinkled.

The stars are so far away that if you telephoned someone on one of those stars it would take four hundred years just for their phone to ring. Then they would answer it, or eat it, depending upon what they do on that star, but you wouldn't be able to hear it for yet another four hundred years, assuming you don't hang up.

The moon, however, is much closer.

The night was clear. Johnny sat on the fire hydrant in front of his house. There was only half a moon. The other half must have been in China.

Johnny looked to the distant stars and beyond. "What is love?" he asked. The stars twinkled.

"Love?" repeated the moon. "You want to know what love is? I'll tell you what love is—pig slop! I'll tell you what love is all right. You've come to the right place, all right. I see lovers every day, from all over the world, with their stupid grins and their silly faces, all talking about how romantic the moon is. I could just spit on them!"

Johnny grinned. "What's it like to be in love?" he asked. The stars twinkled.

"It's like waiting a half an hour for your little sister to get out of the bathroom," answered the moon. "It's like chewing gum while you're eating a chocolate chip cookie. Do you understand what I'm saying? It's like walking around with a garbage can over your head. It's like eating your socks."

"Well, how do you know when you're in love?" asked Johnny. The stars twinkled.

"Oh, you bump into things a lot," said the moon. "You talk to mirrors. You sing a lot of stupid songs. If you find yourself doing stuff like that, then you know you're in love."

"Have you ever been in love?" asked Johnny.

"Me!" exclaimed the moon. "Are you kidding? What kind of sucker do you take me for? I don't go for that pig slop! What do you think, I'm made of green cheese? Have I ever been in love? Hah! What a laugh! What a—" Then the moon heaved a deep sigh and answered in a sad, dreamy voice, "Well, actually, once, yes."

The stars twinkled.

Johnny hopped off of the fire hydrant and started back inside.

"Hey, wait a second!" called the moon. "What're all these questions about love? You're not in love, are you?"

Johnny didn't answer. He walked toward the door.

"It's nothing but hog swill!" yelled the moon.

Johnny opened the front door.

"I hope you like walking around with a garbage can over your head!" called the moon.

Johnny stepped inside and closed the door.

"Go eat your socks!" hollered the moon.

Johnny lay on his bed and stared at the ceiling. "Love sounds wonderful," he thought. His eyes twinkled.

CHAPTER 14

Other Bottle Caps

"There's only one thing worse than working," said Harry Laxatayl, "and that's not working."

The Laxatayls were eating dinner around the kitchen table.

"Peas again!" thought Johnny. "Every night; peas!"

"You'll find a job soon, dear," said Carol. "One where they will appreciate you."

"You could be a pirate," suggested Christene, "or an astronaut."

Harry rubbed his beard. "Maybe I'll be a bull-fighter," he said.

"Oh, Johnny," said his mother. "Louie, from Louie's Lunch Wagon, gave me all of his bottle caps for the week."

"Terrific!" said Johnny. "How many—"

"Honey," interrupted Harry. "I thought we agreed last night not to do that anymore."

"What? Do what?" asked Johnny.

"Oh, but he was so happy to give them to me. You should have seen his smile. He'd been saving them all week for me. I couldn't just say no."

"I don't like it any better than you," said Harry. "It's hard. But you'll have to say no sometime."

"I know. You're right," said Carol. "I just hate to have to do it."

"So do I," said her husband. "But it's got to be done."

"What?" asked Johnny. "What are you talking about?"

"Now isn't the time to disucss it," said his mother. "We'll talk about it after dinner."

"Discuss what?" asked Johnny. "Talk about what after dinner?"

"Eat your peas," replied his mother.

Johnny was worried. Something bad was coming.

The rest of the dinner was eaten in silence. Johnny couldn't eat another bite. He pushed his food around the edges of the plate so that it looked as if there were less.

He cleared the table, ready to start washing the dishes.

"That's all right," said his mother. "You don't have to do them tonight. I'll wash them later."

"Uh oh," thought Johnny. "It's going to be real bad."

They walked into the living room. Johnny sat on the armchair. His parents sat on the couch.

Johnny was scared. He didn't even know what it was and he already felt as if he were going to cry.

His father looked him in the eye, man to man, and said "Son, your mother and I have agreed that you shouldn't have any more bottle caps."

Johnny bit the insides of his mouth and squeezed the chair. "Why not?" he asked. He didn't whine.

"You're too old for them," said his mother. "You're not a little kid anymore. It's silly."

"Those things will take over the whole house if we don't put a stop to it," said his father.

"Well, what about the bottle caps I already have?" he asked, digging his fingernails into the chair.

His father took a deep breath. He hated having to say it. "We're going to have to get rid of them, Johnny," he said.

Johnny couldn't believe it. It was the best bottle cap collection in the world. They couldn't just get rid of it, just like that. There had to be a way out.

"I'm sorry," said his mother.

"I'm sorry," said his father.

"Wait!" exclaimed Johnny. "I have an idea! What about Christene? She's not too old for them. She can have them. Then we can still keep them! Right?"

His parents looked at each other.

"I don't see why not," said his mother.

"It's fine with me," said his father. "Christene, would you like Johnny's bottle cap collection?"

Christene was under the coffee table. "No thanks," she said.

Johnny couldn't believe it.

"I'm afraid she doesn't want them," said his father.

"Wait," said Johnny. "I want to talk with Christene for a second. Wait here. C'mon, Christene."

Christene followed Johnny into his bedroom.

Johnny closed the door.

"All right, listen, Christene," he said. "You don't have to really want my bottle caps. All you have to do is *say* that you want them. Nothing will change. All right?"

Christene shook her head.

"Why not?" Johnny pleaded. "You won't even have to look at them if you don't want to. It will be no different than it is now. Do you like the way it is now?"

"It's okay," said Christene.

"Good," said Johnny. "Then just tell Daddy that you want the bottle caps. Say, 'Daddy, I want a bottle cap collection.'"

Christene shook her head. "No," she said.

Johnny took a deep breath. "Listen closely, Christene. I like the bottle caps. I like them a lot. But

Daddy will get rid of them unless you tell him that you want them. Do you understand?"

Christene shook her head.

"What don't you understand?" demanded Johnny.

Christene shrugged her shoulders.

Johnny paced around the room and tried to think of some way to get through to her.

"What's this?" asked Christene, picking up a bottle on Johnny's desk.

Johnny took the bottle from her. "It's paint remover," he said.

"What would happen if I drank it?" asked Christene.

Johnny read the label. "You'd get real sick," he said. "It should be kept out of the reach of little kids." He stood on his bed and put the bottle of paint remover on his bookshelf.

"What's a reach?" asked Christene. "Do I have one?"

"You shouldn't drink anything unless you know what it is," Johnny said.

"That's silly," said Christene.

"No, I'm serious," said Johnny. "Don't drink anything unless you know what it is."

"I know what shoe polish is," said Christene. "That doesn't mean I can drink it!"

"No, that's not what I meant," said Johnny.

"I know what perfume is, but I'm still not allowed to drink it." She walked out of Johnny's room and called, "Mommy, what's a reach?"

"Wait!" called Johnny. "We still haven't figured out what to do with the bottle cap collection." He ran after her and into the living room where his parents were waiting.

He decided to take a chance. "Christene wants a bottle cap collection!" he announced.

"Is that true, Princess?" asked her mother. "Would you like a bottle cap collection?"

"Okay," said Christene.

A big grin appeared on Johnny's face.

"But not Johnny's bottle cap collection," said Christene. "I don't like those. I want other bottle caps."

Johnny felt his heart slowly sink beneath the floor.

CHAPTER 15

How?

Valerie sneaked into her parents' bedroom, followed by Popover. She opened a dresser drawer, took something out, and stuck it in her pants pocket. She closed the drawer and turned around just as her father entered the room.

She froze.

"Now, what are you up to?" asked her father.

"Hi, Daddy," said Valerie. She edged away from the dresser and sat down on the bed.

"What are you looking so guilty about?" asked her father.

"I'm not looking guilty," said Valerie, as she put her hand over the bulge in her pants pocket.

Popover jumped up onto the bed next to her.

"You're up to something," said her father. "You look like you did that time you convinced Violet that one of her ears was longer than the other."

Violet was Valerie's sister.

"Well, she's older than me. She shouldn't be so stupid," said Valerie.

"She wouldn't leave the house for three days," said her father. "Your mother and I had no idea what was the matter."

"I finally told you, didn't I?" said Valerie.

Valerie's mother walked in.

Valerie quickly changed the subject. "May I invite a friend over to dinner on Tuesday after dance class?"

"I suppose," said her mother.

"Well, so you actually made a friend at dancing school," said her father. "I thought you told me that only clucks go to dance class."

"What's her name?" asked her mother.

"His name is Johnny Laxatayl," said Valerie.

"Oh, I see," smirked her father.

"You don't see anything," said Valerie. "Can I invite him?"

"I said yes," said her mother. "Is that the boy who collects bottle caps?"

"Uh huh," said Valerie.

"I've got a whole bagful for him," said her mother. "All my friends have been collecting them since I told them about it. It's fun."

"Bottle caps, eh?" said her father. "I used to collect gum wrappers when I was a kid. I had quite a collection."

"Big deal," said Valerie. "He's got a whole basement full of bottle caps."

Mrs. Plum gave the bag of bottle caps to Valerie, who then walked over to Johnny's. On her way she passed the Duckermans'.

Donald was out front playing with dirt. "Hey you!" he called. "You're Valerie, aren't you?"

Valerie looked at him. "That's right," she said.

"I thought so," said Donald.

"Do you know me?" asked Valerie.

"I talked to you once before," said Donald. "I could never forget your face."

"Oh?" said Valerie.

"Uh huh," said Donald. "It's too ugly." He laughed. "No matter how hard I try, I just can't forget it!" He laughed some more.

"You must be Donald Duckerman," said Valerie.

"That's me," said Donald.

Valerie shook her head. "You are so immature," she said.

"I am not!" said Donald.

"Are too!" said Valerie.

"How old are you?" Donald demanded.

"Ten," said Valerie.

"I'm ten, too," said Donald. "When's your birthday?"

"December eleventh," said Valerie.

"Mine's October twenty-third," said Donald. "I'm older that you are."

"So, that doesn't mean anything," said Valerie. "You're still immature. Girls mature faster than boys, Cluckerman."

"They do not," said Donald.

"Do too," said Valerie. "Girls are much more mature than boys. I read it in a book."

"What book?" Donald demanded.

"I don't know. It's in about every book ever written," said Valerie.

"I've never read it," said Donald.

"That's because you don't know how to read," said Valerie. "In fact, there's a book at my house now. It's full of all kinds of important stuff and it says that girls are more mature than boys. In fact, it's the very first sentence."

"It must be a joke book," said Donald.

"A seven-year-old girl is as smart as a ten-year-old boy," declared Valerie.

"Where'd you get that one?" asked Donald.

"It's a known fact," said Valerie. "Everybody knows it."

"Well, I don't know it," said Donald.

"See, that proves it," said Valerie. She quickly turned and walked toward Johnny's. She was halfway there when she got hit on the head with a dirt clod. She turned and said, "How immature, Cluckerman."

Then she walked on. She was hit by another dirt clod.

She rang the Laxatayl doorbell.

Christene answered the door.

"Is Johnny home?" asked Valerie.

"Yes," said Christene. She closed the door.

Valerie rang again.

"Now what?" asked Christene.

Valerie stepped inside, went into the hall closet, and down to the greatest bottle cap collection in the world.

Johnny was sitting on his favorite pile of bottle caps. He sadly looked up at Valerie.

"Hi, Johnny," she greeted him. "I brought you some more bottle caps."

Johnny looked down. "Keep 'em," he said.

Valerie was stunned. She had never seen him so sad. "What's the matter?" she asked.

"My parents are getting rid of the bottle cap collection," said Johnny. "They say I'm too old for them, now."

"They can't do that!" exclaimed Valerie. She couldn't believe it. It was the greatest bottle cap collection in the world. "Why?" she asked.

"I don't know," said Johnny. "I don't know."

"There's got to be something we can do!" declared Valerie.

"There's nothing," said Johnny. "I tried."

Valerie paced around the basement and tried to think of something.

Her eyes lit up as she stopped pacing. She smiled, then just said one word: "How?"

"What?" asked Johnny.

"How?" Valerie repeated. "How are they going to get rid of them?"

"I don't know," muttered Johnny. "It doesn't matter."

Valerie smiled. "They can't do it," she said. "It's impossible. You have too many of them!"

"Really?" asked Johnny.

"There's no way!" Valerie insisted. "It can't be

done! It's the world's greatest bottle cap collection. Nothing can destroy it!"

A smile slowly formed on Johnny's face. He couldn't think of a way to get rid of them. It was the world's greatest bottle cap collection and nothing could destroy it. He beamed at Valerie. She had done it. She had saved his bottle cap collection—or so it seemed. He picked up a bottle cap, snapped his fingers, and sent it sailing across the room. "I did it!" he exclaimed.

Valerie gave him the bottle caps her mother's friends had collected. Johnny tossed them in the air, letting them fall all around the basement.

Valerie laughed. "I brought something else, too," she said mysteriously.

"What?" asked Johnny.

Valerie reached into her pocket and pulled out a pack of cigarettes.

Johnny gulped. "W-wh-where'd you get tho-those?" he asked.

"I stole them from home," replied Valerie.

Johnny was truly amazed. He stared at the cigarettes. He hated cigarettes, or at least he used to hate cigarettes. He liked Valerie. She had just saved his bottle cap collection, maybe.

Valerie tore open the pack of cigarettes with her teeth, then handed one to Johnny.

Johnny took it. He looked at Valerie and fumbled with his cigarette. He thought she was amazing. He tore the cigarette in half. "Oops," he said.

Valerie laughed. She gave him another one and took one for herself. "Relax," she said.

"Don't they have cancer?" asked Johnny.

"Don't be immature," said Valerie.

Valerie struck a match, then lit the wrong end of her cigarette. "Oops," she said.

Johnny laughed. "Relax," he said. He took the matches from her, lit his cigarette, and breathed in. "Uhgk gack hack kaw!" he coughed.

Valerie laughed. She lit a new cigarette. "Agh kuck ucha!" she gasped.

Johnny laughed.

They sat in the basement, coughing and laughing, but after a while they stopped laughing and just coughed.

Johnny felt sick.

Valerie's cigarette was almost finished. "I don't feel too good," she said. "Ucha kawk!" She was very pale. She snuffed out her cigarette in a bottle cap and got up. Then she darted up the stairs.

Johnny didn't feel any better and he looked even worse. He put his cigarette out, stood up, stumbled, then ran up the stairs after her. He ran out of the hall closet, through the front door which Valerie had left open, and outside into the fresh air. He watched Valerie Plum run away up the street.

He leaned against the fire hydrant. She had saved his bottle cap collection—hadn't she?

The cigarettes remained behind a pile of bottle caps in the basement. Luckily, nobody else ever went down there.

The sky was grey. It looked as if it might rain, but the fresh air felt good.

CHAPTER 16

One at a Time

There once was a Russian author named Leo Tolstoy who wrote a magnificent book that was over three thousand pages long. Some people think it's the best book ever written. When someone once asked him, "Leo, how did you write such a magnificent book?" the great Russian writer replied, "One word at a time."

Johnny leaned against the fire hydrant in front of his house. He felt good and bad. He felt good because Valerie had just saved his bottle cap collection. He felt sick because he had just smoked a cigarette.

"Hey, Johnny! Whatcha doin'?" called Donald from across the street.

"Nothin'," said Johnny.

Donald kicked a rock against the fire hydrant and walked after it. "What is the matter with Valerie?" he asked.

"Who?" asked Johnny.

"Valerie," said Donald. "She went running past my house just now." He smiled broadly. "She looked terrible."

"She had to go home," said Johnny.

"She's kind of dumb, huh?" asked Donald.

"I don't know," said Johnny. "She just saved my bottle cap collection."

"Huh?" asked Donald.

"My parents said I have to get rid of the bottle caps. They think I'm too old for them."

"They're wrong," said Donald.

"It's all right," said Johnny. "Valerie figured it out. I have too many bottle caps. They can't get rid of them. It's impossible. It's the greatest bottle cap collection in the world. They can't get rid of it!"

Donald picked up his rock and put it in his pocket. "They can do it," he said.

"What?" asked Johnny.

"They can get rid of 'em, all right," said Donald.

"How?" asked Johnny.

"It's simple," said Donald.

"How?" Johnny asked again.

"Easy," said Donald.

"How?" pleaded Johnny.

"One bottle cap at a time," said Donald.

A raindrop fell on Johnny's forehead. Another hit his shoulder. "Come on," said Donald. "We better go inside." Johnny didn't move. The raindrops hit him one at a time, but before too long he was fairly wet.

Johnny followed Donald to the door. "One at a time," he thought.

"She thinks she's so smart all the time," said Donald. "What did you and Valerie do, anyway?"

"Nothing," Johnny muttered. "Smoked a cigarette."

"You smoked a cigarette!" exclaimed Donald.

Johnny, realizing he had impressed Donald, just shrugged his shoulders. "Sure," he said, as if it were nothing.

"Wow!" said Donald.

Johnny smiled.

"I don't believe you," challenged Donald.

"We did," Johnny insisted.

"Prove it," said Donald.

"Okay," said Johnny. "Come on." He led Donald

down to the basement. "There they are, over there!" pointed Johnny.

Donald stared at the cigarettes. His face took on a curious expression. "Let's smoke one," he said.

Johnny turned pale. "No, you're too immature," he said.

"That was Valerie's word," thought Donald. Johnny had never used that word before. "I am not," he said aloud. "I'm only four months younger than you, and I'm older than Valerie."

Johnny began to feel sick again. "It's got nothing to do with how old you are," he said. "They have cancer."

"I'm not scared," said Donald.

Johnny's hands were sweating. "It's got nothing to do with being scared."

"Come on," said Donald. "If Valerie could do it, so can I."

They sat down on the bottle caps. Johnny's hands were shaking. He held his breath, gave Donald a cigarette, and took one for himself.

"What do I do?" asked Donald.

"It's just like on TV," Johnny answered.

Donald struck a match and lit his cigarette.

Johnny lit his. "Ach gah kaw!" he coughed.

Donald didn't cough. He looked a little funny but he didn't cough. He just puffed along.

"Ackah hack!" coughed Johnny.

Donald gave Johnny a funny look.

Johnny felt sick. "Ukha!"

At last it was over. Johnny wiped his forehead with his sleeve.

Donald looked funny. "Let's smoke another one," he said.

Johnny figured one more couldn't make him feel any worse than he already felt. He smoked another one, one puff at a time, until at last it was through.

"I don't get it," said Donald, when he finished. "I must be doing something wrong. One more."

One more.

Somewhere in the middle of that third cigarette, Johnny didn't cough as much, and he began to feel a little better. He didn't feel good but he didn't feel sick either. He felt nothing, which was the best he'd felt in a while.

Donald finished his cigarette and snuffed it out in a bottle cap. "I don't get it," he said. "You and Valerie did this?"

Johnny felt nothing. "Sure, we do it all the time," he said.

"That's stupid," said Donald. "It's disgusting. They taste terrible. They smell awful. And they make you sick. That's really stupid. I just don't get it."

He walked up the stairs and outside. It was still raining, but not too hard. Donald liked it that way.

Johnny stepped outside. He took a deep breath, then suddenly ran inside, into the bathroom, and threw up.

Donald took his rock out of his pocket and walked back up the street, kicking it along. Some people like to smoke. Donald liked to walk in the rain and kick rocks.

CHAPTER 17

Some Good News

Bad dreams are better than good dreams.

When you have a bad dream, you wake up, you look around, and you say, "Whew! It was only a dream. Everything is still the same as it was—wonderful!

When you have a good dream, you wake up, you look around, and you say, "Darn! It was only a dream. Everything is still the same as it was—rotten."

The night after Johnny smoked the cigarettes, he had all kinds of horrible dreams.

He dreamed that he was a pencil. And that he had a dull point. So he went into a pencil sharpener and it sharpened him and sharpened him, but he still just had the same dull point. It sharpened and sharpened, and he got smaller and smaller, and the point remained dull. Pretty soon, all that was left of him was his eraser and his dull point.

He woke up. He looked around. He felt the top of his head. It felt pointy. "Whew, he said, "it was only a dream. Everything is still the same as it was—wonderful."

He dreamed he was walking down the street in front of his house, only the street was a little bit different. It had a big tree in the middle of it, the same tree that was in the middle of the Duckerman's basketball court.

As he walked down that street, he felt a rock hit him in the back. He turned around, but there was nobody there. He continued walking, and was hit by another rock. Again, nobody was there. Another rock flew by him. They were coming from behind the tree!

He ran toward the tree, dodging rocks. He got to the tree and looked behind it. There stood Valerie Plum and Donald Duckerman, each holding a handful of rocks.

"Hi, Johnny," said Valerie. "What's the matter?"

"Someone threw a rock at me," said Johnny.

Valerie laughed.

"I wonder who could have done it?" said Donald.

"I don't know," said Johnny. "It came from behind this tree."

"Well, I didn't see anyone back here except for Valerie," said Donald.

"And I didn't see anyone except for Donald," said Valerie.

Donald and Valerie looked at each other and laughed.

"Well, if you see anyone, let me know," said Johnny. He walked away. A rock hit him in the back and he woke up.

He looked around. "Whew, it was only a dream. Everything is still as wonderful as ever!"

He dreamed the house was on fire and that he was trapped inside. The firemen came and extinguished the blaze, but he was still trapped inside. All the windows and doors had been burnt away.

He woke up, looked around, and realized everything was still wonderful. "Whew," he sighed.

He dreamed that his bottle caps were taken away, one at a time, by an army of ants, each ant carrying one bottle cap on its back.

He woke up and looked around. It was a wonderful world.

Then he had a wonderful dream. He was king of the world, or was it the moon? And Valerie Plum was queen.

When he woke up, he looked around and said, "Rats! It was only a lousy dream. Everything is still the same as it was—rotten.

It was after ten o'clock in the morning. He got out of bed and went into the kitchen.

"Morning," said his father. "I have some good news for you."

"What?" grumbled Johnny. He wondered how there could be good news in a rotten world.

"We don't have to throw away your bottle caps," said his father.

Johnny felt his heart rise up from beneath the floor. Things were pretty good after all. "That's really great," he said. "That really is good news."

"We're going to sell them," continued his father.

Johnny felt as if he'd been hit by a rock.

"We're selling them to the Metal Press," said his father. "I talked to a fellow there this morning, a man by the name of Daggert. He seemed like a real fair man, very polite. He said they will give us one and a half cents a pound for them."

"No!" said Johnny. "I don't want money for them! I'd rather throw them away. Please. I don't want to sell them to the Metal Press."

"Don't be silly," said his father. "They are willing to give you a penny and a half a pound for them. And they will even haul them out of the basement themselves for a minimal charge."

"How much is a half a penny?" asked Christene.

"It's half of a penny," replied her father.

"Oh," said Christene. "What's niminal?"

"Mi-ni-mal," corrected her father. "It means small."

"It sure is a big word for meaning small," said Christene.

"I don't want to sell them!" Johnny insisted.

"I've already made the arrangements," said his father. "They'll be coming Thursday morning." That was only four days away. "Don't worry. You'll get to keep all the money."

"I think a penny and a half sounds pretty minimal," said Christene.

CHAPTER 18

Popover Plum

After dance class, Johnny and Valerie raced on their bikes to Valerie's, where Johnny was invited for dinner. Valerie had an advantage since Johnny didn't know the way. Whenever he got in the lead, Valerie would turn off on some side street and yell, "This way!" Johnny would have to turn back around and go after her.

"I won!" called Valerie as she hopped off her bycycle.

"Look out!" Johnny shouted. "I don't have any brakes!" He whizzed past her and smashed into the side of her garage.

Valerie led Johnny into her house.

Mrs. Plum met them in the hallway. She stopped and stared at Johnny.

Valerie introduced them. "Mom, this is Johnny Laxatayl. Johnny, this is my mother."

"Pleased to meet you," said Johnny.

"How do you do," said Mrs. Plum as she continued staring at him.

It made Johnny feel uneasy.

"Have I met you before?" she finally asked.

"No," said Johnny. "I don't think so."

"Are you sure?" asked Mrs. Plum. "You look strangely familiar."

"You haven't met him," stated Valerie.

"He looks very familiar," said her mother.

"No he doesn't," insisted Valerie. "Come on, Johnny."

She led Johnny past her mother and on into the living room. Valerie's father looked up from his newspaper. "You must be Johnny Laxatayl," he said, then winked at Valerie.

"Johnny, I'd like you to meet my father."

Johnny and Mr. Plum shook hands.

Mr. Plum sat back down. "We've met before, haven't we?" he asked as he relit his pipe.

"I don't think so," said Johnny. "I think I have a familiar face."

Mr. Plum stared and puffed on the pipe. "No, I've seen you around," he said. "Were you ever one of my students?"

Mr. Plum was a professor at the college.

"He's just going into the sixth grade!" said Valerie. "You've never seen him before."

"You don't know everybody I've seen," said her father. "I know I know him from somewhere."

"No you don't!" said Valerie. "You don't know what you're talking about."

Johnny cocked his head.

"I know that face!" said Mr. Plum.

"No you don't!" said Valerie. "Come on, Johnny. Let's go to my room."

Mr. Plum watched Johnny walk down the hall.

Violet met them in front of Valerie's room. "Well, Valerie," she said, "who's your cute boyfriend?"

Johnny blushed.

Valerie introduced them. "Violet, this is Johnny. Johnny, this is my ugly sister."

Violet looked Johnny over. "I know you," she said. "No I don't. You look like somebody. Who do you look like?"

Johnny shrugged his shoulders. "Everybody says I look like my Uncle Joe," he said.

Violet paid no attention to him. "Who do you look like?" She snapped her fingers. "I know you look like someone." She snapped her fingers. "Who?"

"Hey, Violet," interrupted Valerie, "What's that on your neck?"

Violet moved her hand toward her neck.

"Don't touch it!" warned Valerie.

Violet's hand stopped.

Johnny didn't see anything on her neck.

"I don't feel—" began Violet.

"Shh!" said Valerie. "Keep perfectly still and don't say a word. Maybe it will go away."

She quietly led Johnny into her room, then slammed the door with a loud bang.

"Ah!" gasped Violet from the other side of the door. "You little rat!"

Johnny and Valerie laughed. Johnny looked around the room. Everything in it was purple, the walls, the bed, the curtains. He sat on the purple carpet. "I must look like somebody your family knows," he said.

"Oh, they're just stupid!" said Valerie. "Oh, wait. I almost forgot. I got some more bottle caps. I was going to bring them to dance class but then I remembered you were coming to dinner. I'll go get them. Wait here." She left the room.

Johnny sat on the floor and frowned. He hadn't yet told her that the bottle caps were being sold to the Metal Press.

Popover walked in and sniffed Johnny.

Johnny stared at Popover.

Popover stared at Johnny.

They both cocked their heads.

Valerie returned with a bag of bottle caps. "That's Popo," she said.

Johnny petted Popover. "Nice-looking dog," he said.

Valerie smiled. She sat down across from Johnny with Popover in between. They both petted him.

"My father is going to sell the bottle caps to the Metal Press," said Johnny. "They're coming Thursday to get them."

Valerie smiled. "What are you worried about? Don't you remember? It's the world's greatest bottle cap collection. No one can take it away. It's impossible!"

"Donald Duckerman figured out how," said Johnny.

"Donald Duckerman's a cluck," said Valerie.

"He told me how they can get rid of the bottle caps," said Johnny.

"How?" demanded Valerie.

"One bottle cap at a time," said Johnny.

Valerie fell over laughing. "Are you kidding?" she asked. "That's got to be the dumbest thing I ever heard!"

"One bottle cap at a time," sighed Johnny.

"You have over a million bottle caps," said Valerie. "If they took them out one bottle cap at a time, it would take over fifty years to get rid of them."

"Hey! That's right!" said Johnny. "They can't do it."

"You have too many," said Valerie. "One bottle cap at a time! What a cluck!"

Johnny laughed. He smiled at Valerie. She'd done it again. She'd saved his bottle cap collection.

Popover wagged his tail.

Mrs. Plum called the children to dinner.

They had pot roast, mashed potatoes, and peas. All the Plums kept staring at Johnny. Violet was snapping her fingers. For the first time in his life, Johnny liked the peas. Perhaps it was the way Mrs. Plum cooked them, or maybe it had something to do with Valerie, but Johnny liked the peas. He really liked them.

After dinner, Johnny and Valerie returned to Valerie's room, followed by Popover.

Popover kept staring at Johnny. Johnny stared back

at Popover. "Your dog looks strangely familiar," he said.

"I guess all dogs look alike," said Valerie.

"I guess," said Johnny.

Popover stared at Johnny and cocked his head.

"I look like your dog!" exclaimed Johnny.

Valerie laughed. She didn't mean to. It was the wrong thing to do.

"I look like your dog," muttered Johnny in disbelief. He stood up and walked out of her room. He didn't want to look like her dog. He went outside and picked up Zordtch.

Valerie ran out after him. "What's wrong with looking like my dog?" she asked.

"Shut up!" said Johnny. He hopped on Zordtch and rode away.

"I like my dog!" Valerie called after him.

Violet had overheard them. "Do you want to know who he looks like?" she announced to her parents. "He looks like Popover!"

They all laughed.

Johnny rode home. He had a terrible taste in his mouth. It must have been the peas.

CHAPTER 19

The Metal Press

A short, fat, ugly man sat at a short, fat, ugly desk puffing on a short, fat, smelly cigar. At the other end of the room a tall, young, handsome man sat tall at a handsome, polished desk.

In the center of the room was a huge, terrible, contraption that wheezed and snorted.

On the door to the room were the following words:

Scaggs' and Daggert's
Metal Press

A little girl walked up to the door carrying a shopping bag full of doorknobs. The tall, young, handsome man rose from his seat and let her in, nice and polite.

The girl stood there a moment and then asked, "How much will you give me for my doorknobs?"

"Put them on the scale," said the short, fat, ugly man.

There was a big scale in the corner. The little girl set the bag on the scale.

The short, fat, ugly man puffed on his cigar. "Twenty-five cents each," he said.

"That's all?" asked the girl. "Doorknobs are hard to

collect. Most people only have enough for their doors. It took me my whole life to get these."

"The scale doesn't lie," the man replied.

The girl looked at the floor.

"Wait," said the tall, young, handsome man. "I'll see what I can do for you." He walked over to the other man. "What do you say, Scaggs?" he asked. "Can we give her a little more?"

"The scale doesn't lie, Daggert," replied Scaggs.

"It took her all her life to collect them," said Daggert. "Come on. Just this once."

"Daggert, you are too nice of a guy," said Scaggs. "All right, thirty cents each."

The tall, young, handsome man walked back to the little girl with the good news. "Thirty cents each," he told her. "As it is, we are losing money on the deal. We've got to keep in business, too."

"Okay," said the girl. "I don't want you to have to go out of business."

The Metal Press snorted.

The short, fat, ugly man puffed on his cigar.

The tall, young, handsome man picked up the bag of doorknobs and dumped them through a hole on the side of the Metal Press.

It chomped and wheezed.

A thin, flat sheet of metal slid out the other side.

"That's your doorknobs," said Scaggs.

"And here is your thirty cents," said Daggert. He held out three dimes.

The girl didn't take them. "You said thirty cents *each*," she said. "I had over fifty doorknobs in that bag."

"Thirty cents *each bagful*," explained Daggert. "I hope you didn't think we meant thirty cents each doorknob."

The girl nodded her head.

The two men laughed. The Metal Press snorted.

"Well, we certainly don't want to cheat her, now, do we, Scaggs?" asked Daggert.

Scaggs shook his short, fat, ugly head.

"You can have your doorknobs back, or what's left of them, anyway," said Daggert, holding out the thin, flat sheet of metal. "Unless you would rather have the thirty cents."

"They're no good to me now," said the girl. She took the thirty cents.

"Glad to be of service," said Daggert. He held the door open for her, nice and polite.

The Metal Press snorted.

A boy walked through the door wheeling a red wagon. "Do you want to buy my wagon?" he asked.

"Put it on the scale," said the short, fat, ugly man.

The boy put it on the scale.

"We'll give you ten cents for it," said the short, fat, ugly man.

"Ten cents!" exclaimed the boy. "It's worth at least two dollars."

"The scale doesn't lie," said the short, fat, ugly man. "Ten cents, take it or leave it."

The boy looked as if he were going to cry.

Daggert winked at him. "I'll see what I can do," he said. He walked over to the other man. "What do you say, Scaggs?" he asked.

"You're too nice of a guy, Daggert," said Scaggs.

The tall, young, handsome man returned to the boy. "I can get you twenty cents for it," he said.

"But it's worth two dollars," said the boy.

"The scale doesn't lie," said Daggert. "It's only worth ten cents. I got you double."

The Metal Press snorted.

"Double?" asked the boy.

"Double," Daggert assured him.

"Okay," said the boy.

The tall, young, handsome man put the wagon through the hole in the Metal Press.

It chomped and wheezed.

A thin, flat, red sheet of metal slid out the other side.

"There's your wagon," laughed Scaggs.

"And here's your twenty cents," said Daggert.

The boy didn't move. Tears filled his eyes. "That was my favorite toy," he said. "But my mother lost her job and we need the money."

"Good. Glad to be able to help out," said Daggert.

The boy didn't move. "Twenty cents won't go very far," he said.

"You want more money?" asked Scaggs. "Bring in more wagons."

The Metal Press snorted.

The boy grabbed his twenty cents and started toward the door. The tall, young, handsome, man held it open for him. The short, fat, ugly man puffed on his cigar. "Hey, kid," he called. "You want to earn five dollars? Be here tomorrow at eight in the morning. I'll give you a job."

"Sure!" said the boy.

"Scaggs, you are too nice of a guy," said Daggert.

"Just like you, Daggert," he replied. "Just like you."

"Wait a second," said the boy. "What will I have to do?"

"Nothing much," said Scaggs. "Just help us get rid of a few bottle caps."

CHAPTER 20

Five Dollars

Early the next morning, Johnny was in the basement. He looked around at his bottle caps, possibly for the last time. "I look like Valerie's dog," he told them.

It didn't make any sense that the people from the Metal Press were going to come and try to take away his bottle caps. It just wasn't fair. He picked up a handful of bottle caps and threw them at the wall. They were too light. They only made it halfway before fluttering down. A penny and a half a pound. It didn't make any sense.

Valerie thought it was impossible. She said it was the greatest bottle cap collection in the world. No one could get rid of it. But what did she know? She was stupid. And so was her ugly dog!

He saw the pack of cigarettes lying in the corner. He picked it up and stuck it in his sock so that no one would find it.

"Popo," he thought. "What a dumb name for a dog!"

He heard a truck come snorting down the street. "They're here," he uttered, and took a deep breath.

It's not fair! Johnny looked around, then started

stuffing his pockets with bottle caps. "It's not fair!" he cried.

The truck wheezed to a halt in front of his house. A short, fat, ugly man stepped out followed by a tall, young, handsome man and a little boy.

The boy was smiling. These were the same men who had turned his wagon into a flat sheet of scrap metal, yet he was smiling. Well, after all, they were paying him five dollars.

The tall man opened the rear of the truck. He pulled out rope, pulleys, a ramp, a wheelbarrow, some cloth sacks, and a shovel.

It was an ugly shovel. It wasn't even dirty. It had never been used to plant a tree or transplant a rosebush. A clean shovel is an ugly shovel.

The two men lifted the scale and set it on the sidewalk. *The scale always lied.*

Johnny's parents went out to greet them. Everyone shook hands and smiled.

The men took their equipment into the house and began to set it up.

The boy took the shovel down to the basement. Johnny was sitting on the bottom step.

"Hello," said the boy.

Johnny didn't answer.

When the boy saw the bottle caps, he dropped the shovel and stared around in amazement. He walked around the basement on top of all the bottle caps.

The short, fat, ugly man came down the stairs. "Look out, Kid," he said as he stepped past Johnny.

Johnny didn't look out.

The man hooked up a series of pulleys along the stairs and strung the rope through them.

The boy picked up his shovel and the operation began. He dug his shovel into the bottle caps and filled up one of the cloth sacks.

The man took the sack and hooked it onto the rope. Then he hoisted it up the stairs as if he were raising a flag on a flagpole. "Here we go, Daggert," he called.

The tall, young, handsome man received the bag at the top of the stairs. "Got it, Scaggs," he called. He unhooked it and put it in his wheelbarrow. He wheeled it outside, down the ramp, and out to the scale on the sidewalk.

Harry Laxatayl went with him to make sure the sack was weighed correctly. They weighed the sack, wrote the weight down on a sheet of paper, then dumped out the bottle caps in the back of the truck.

The tall, young, handsome man wheeled the empty wheelbarrow back up the ramp and inside, into the hall closet. He returned just as the short, fat, ugly man said, "Coming again, Daggert."

"Right here, Scaggs," he replied. He unhooked the full bag and sent the empty one back down.

And so the operation was repeated, again and again and again.

And again.

"Why are you helping them?" Johnny asked the boy. "Why?"

"Five dollars," said the boy.

"Five dollars?!" exclaimed Johnny. "But this is the greatest bottle cap collection in the world!"

"Sure is!" agreed the boy.

"Well, then, why are you doing it?" Johnny asked.

"Five dollars," was all the boy could say.

"Hey, Boy, get back to work!" ordered Scaggs.

The boy filled another sack and Scaggs hooked it on the rope and hoisted it up the stairs. "Coming up, Daggert," he called.

"Keep 'em coming, Scaggs," was the reply.

Outside, Christene climbed up onto the scale. It only registered twenty-eight pounds.

Harry and Daggert were coming out the front door. When Daggert saw Christene on the scale, he yelled, "Hey! Get off there!" He gave the wheelbarrow to Harry and ran toward Christene. "Get down, little girl," he said.

Harry Laxatayl, whistling, slowly wheeled the wheelbarrow toward them.

"Get down before your father gets here," said Daggert.

"I weigh twenty-eight pounds," bragged Christene.

Daggert began to perspire.

When her father approached, Christene jumped off the scale and into his arms. Harry dropped the wheelbarrow and caught her.

"Do you know how much I weigh, Daddy?" she asked.

"How much, Princess?" asked Harry.

Daggert held his breath.

Christene bit her finger. "I forget," she said.

Daggert exhaled.

"Well, you feel about fifty pounds to me," said Harry, and he set her down.

Daggert weighed the sack of bottlecaps. "Tell your daughter to stay off the scale," he said. "She might hurt herself." He patted Christene's head.

The operation continued.

Throughout the day Johnny's aunts and uncles stopped by to witness the event. But when they got there, they didn't feel like watching. Instead, they stayed in the kitchen where Carol Laxatayl served coffee and cake.

Johnny had moved to a pile of bottle caps in the middle of the basement. It wasn't fair. It didn't make any sense. Nothing made sense anymore.

Donald came over to watch the event. He thought it would be fun. He sat in the basement next to Johnny and watched the bottle caps being shoveled into cloth sacks, then hoisted up the stairs by a short, fat, ugly man. It wasn't fun.

"So what's new?" asked Johnny.

"Oh, nothing," said Donald. "What about you?"

"Oh, you know," said Johnny.

Donald couldn't stand to watch it for very long. He walked back up the steps and on outside. He took a rock from his pocket and threw it against the side of the truck. Then he kicked it on home.

The operation continued late into the afternoon.

Valerie Plum came over because she was worried about Johnny and about what he thought about her now. It was she who had said they couldn't get rid of the bottle caps. She didn't lie. She really thought they couldn't do it.

She was afraid to go down and see him right away so she went into the kitchen with the adults. They asked her how she liked dancing school and if she was excited about going into the sixth grade. "I guess," she answered both times. She ate a piece of cake with a glass of milk, then walked into the hall closet.

She passed a tall, handsome man and stepped down the stairs. She saw a sack full of bottle caps go by and she heard someone say, "Coming your way, Daggert."

When she saw the basement she quickly turned away, then very slowly turned back around. She could just about see the actual basement floor. Johnny still sat on a big pile in the center, but besides them, there wasn't too much left.

"How are you doing?" she asked.

"I guess so," said Johnny.

"That's good," said Valerie. "Well, I have to go now. Will you be all right?"

"Pretty good," said Johnny.

Valerie left.

The boy had gotten all of the bottle caps except for the pile on which Johnny sat.

Johnny got off.

The boy dug his shovel into the pile and filled another sack.

"I got some more," said Johnny. He took the bottle caps out of his pockets and threw them on the pile.

The operation continued.

The operation was completed. The bottle caps were in the truck.

The short, fat, ugly man gathered up the equipment.

The tall, young, handsome man totaled up the figures. There had been eight thousand, four hundred, and twenty-two pounds of bottle caps—according to the scale.

At a penny and a half per pound, he figured a gross total of one hundred and twenty-six dollars, and thirty-three cents ($126.33).

The minimal charge for removing them was forty dollars (40.00).

He subtracted the latter from the former, leaving a final total of eighty-six dollars and thirty-three cents ($86.33).

He paid Johnny the money.

Johnny wadded it up and threw it down the hatch into the basement. He shut the trapdoor.

Then the boy was paid five dollars. He took it and ran away.

The two men returned to their truck, quite pleased with themselves. But then,

"You dummy, Daggert!"

"It was your fault, Scaggs!"

They had gotten a ticket for parking in front of a fire hydrant.

CHAPTER 21

Not in the Basement

The bottle caps were gone. The hatch to the basement was shut tight.

"John-ny! John-ny, where are you? Johnny! Princess, do you know where your brother is? *Johnny!*"

Christene nodded her head.

"*John-ny!* Where are you, Johnny? Johnny? Harry, I'm worried about Johnny. Harry? Harry?? *Harry!*"

"I'm right here," said Harry Laxatayl, who was lying on the couch in the living room. "What's the matter?"

"I'm worried about Johnny," said Carol as she walked into the living room. "I don't know where he is. *John-ny!*"

"Princess, do you know where Johnny is?" asked her father.

Christene nodded her head.

"Well, where is he?" he asked.

"He's not in the basement," said Christene.

"Yes, we know that," said her father. "But do you know where he is?"

Christene nodded her head.

"Where, Princess?" asked her mother.

"Somewhere else," explained Christene.

"Where else?!" asked her father.

"Not in the basement!" said Christene, a little annoyed at having to repeat herself so many times.

"Johnny!" screamed Carol Laxatayl.

Johnny was not in the basement. The hatch was shut tight. The basement was haunted.

"Johnny, where *are* you?"

He was up on the roof. A cigarette dangled from his mouth, although it wasn't lit. He wanted to feel nothing again. "I just can't believe they're gone," he said.

"You keep saying that," said the moon. "What do you want me to do about it? There is nothing I can do about it."

"They're gone," said Johnny.

"So you say," said the moon.

Johnny sucked on his cigarette.

"Believe me, Kid, I feel bad for you," said the moon. "I really do. It was quite a collection. There's no denying it. But it's over now. You had some real tough luck. But now you have to move on."

"It was the greatest bottle cap collection in the world," said Johnny. "They were always there."

"Look, those are the breaks, Kid," said the moon. "Thinking about them won't bring them back. Think about what else you have."

"What else do I have?" asked Johnny. "Valerie doesn't like me, or if she does, it's just because I look like her dog."

"I warned you about that, Kid," said the moon. "I warned you not to fall in love with her. Don't say I didn't warn you."

"Johnny!" called his mother. "Where are you, Johnny?"

"I'm not in love," said Johnny. "I just wish I didn't look like her dog."

"Johnny! *Johnny!*"

"It's not as if you didn't get anything for them," said the moon. "You got eighty-six dollars and thirty-three cents. To be perfectly honest, that was a lot more than I thought you'd get."

"You want it?" asked Johnny.

"I don't have any use for money," said the moon.

"Neither do I," said Johnny.

"Johnny? Are you all right? Where *are* you?"

"Eighty-six dollars and thirty-three cents," Johnny muttered. He threw down his cigarette and stamped on it. "Eighty-six dollars and thirty-three cents. People I didn't even know gave me bottle caps. Now what do I have? Eighty-six dollars and thirty-three cents."

A dog howled.

"You'll get over it," said the moon.

"I don't want to get over it," said Johnny.

The dog howled again.

"Look, I have to go now," said the moon. "That dog's howling to me."

"Go ahead," said Johnny. "I think I heard my mother say something."

He climbed down from the corner of the roof onto a fence, jumped to the ground, and went inside. His mother was in the living room. He walked up behind her.

"Johnny!" she called.

"What?" asked Johnny.

Carol turned around with a start. "Oh, Johnny," she sighed, "you scared me."

"Sorry," said Johnny.

His mother smiled at him. "Are you okay?" she asked. "Do you feel like talking about it? Would you like something to eat?"

"I'm okay," said Johnny.

"I remember when I was a little girl," said his mother. "I had a favorite pillow. It was a clown's face. I used to take it with me, everywhere." She smiled, remembering it. "It had a big fluffy nose, and long eyebrows made out of yarn. But then one day it was gone. I never even found out what happened to it. It was just gone. I think I must have cried for a month. But I got over it."

"I'm not going to cry," said Johnny. "And I'm not going to get over it."

"There's a difference between getting over something, and forgetting something," said his mother. "I haven't forgotten my pillow. It's just that now when I think about it, I smile."

"I guess," said Johnny.

"So, what are you going to do with *all that money?*" asked his mother.

"Nothing," said Johnny.

"Nothing at all?" asked his mother.

"No," said Johnny.

"Well, I think that's okay," said his mother. "Nothing. Yes I think that sounds like a fine idea."

Johnny looked at his mother. "That's too bad about your pillow," he said.

CHAPTER 22

Blood Money

At Aunt Mary's bridge party, all of her friends brought her the bottle caps they had collected for Johnny. They couldn't understand it when she said, "Keep your stinking bottle caps!"

It had been several weeks since the bottle caps were destroyed. The money still lay on the floor of the basement, eighty-six dollars and thirty-three cents. Nobody had been down there since that day. The basement was haunted.

All around, people who knew Johnny, and people who knew somebody who knew Johnny, and even people who knew someone who knew somebody who knew Johnny, were throwing away their bottle caps for the first time in years. It was strangely sad.

"What do you want to do?" asked Johnny. He was sitting on the fire hydrant in front of his house.

"I don't know," answered Donald. He was sitting on the ground next to Johnny, running his fingers through the dirt.

"I wish school didn't have to start so soon," said Johnny.

It seemed as if summer vacation had only just started, but school would begin again in a little over a week. That's a peculiar thing about summer. The days are longer, yet they go by so much quicker.

"I hate school," said Donald.

"Me too," said Johnny.

"I like summer vacation," said Donald.

"Me too," said Johnny.

"Too bad there's nothing to do," said Donald.

Johnny nodded.

Valerie came walking toward them. "Hi, Johnny," she called. Then she saw Donald. "Duckerman," she muttered.

"Plum," replied Donald.

Johnny looked at the two of them from his position on the fire hydrant. It was the first time he had seen them together. When he was with Donald, they'd talk about what a jerk Valerie was. When he was with Valerie, they'd talk about what a cluck Donald was. But now they were all together. He wondered what they'd talk about.

"What's going on?" asked Valerie.

"Nothing," said Johnny. "There's nothing to do."

"You could do a lot with eighty-six dollars and thirty-three cents," said Valerie.

"I don't want that money," said Johnny.

"Why not?" asked Donald.

"I just don't, that's all," said Johnny.

"He's got all that money just sitting in the basement," said Donald. "I wish he'd spend it."

"I know," said Valerie. "That's what I've been trying to tell him for the last three weeks."

"Me too!" exclaimed Donald. "Boy, think of all you can do with eighty-six dollars and thirty-three cents."

"You could have all kinds of fun," said Valerie.

"All kinds," said Donald.

Valerie and Donald looked at each other and smiled.

"That's blood money," said Johnny.

"All money is the same," said Valerie.

"It doesn't matter where you got it," said Donald.

"That's what I've been trying to tell him," said Valerie.

"Me too," said Donald.

Valerie smiled at Donald. Donald smiled back.

"What if someone killed your dog?" asked Johnny. "Would you take money for it?"

Valerie shrugged her shoulders. "I don't know," she said.

"A dog is different from bottle caps," said Donald. "What's so great about a bottle cap?"

Johnny was taken aback by that question. "It was the greatest bottle cap collection in the world!" he declared.

"It was the *only* bottle cap collection in the world," laughed Valerie.

Donald also laughed.

Johnny couldn't believe it. He felt as if he was going to cry.

"What were you ever going to do with them?" asked Donald.

"I, uh, I—" stuttered Johnny.

"It really was kind of silly, when you think about it," said Valerie.

"It was not!" Johnny insisted.

"Think of all you can buy with eighty-six dollars," said Donald.

"And thirty-three cents," added Valerie.

Donald and Valerie lay back on the grass and thought of all the neat stuff they could buy.

Johnny couldn't believe it. "No," he said. "I'm not going to spend that money."

"I know," said Valerie. "You can buy a new bike."

"One that has brakes," said Donald. "Have you ever seen his bike, Val?"

Valerie nodded and laughed.

Johnny couldn't believe it. He thought Zordtch was the best bike in the world, better than any bike he could buy in a store.

"Do you know what you should do?" said Valerie.

"You should sell your old bike to the Metal Press and get even more money. Then you can buy a really slick one."

"I like my bike," said Johnny.

Donald and Valerie laughed.

"Get lost!" said Johnny. "I'm going inside. Get out of here. The Metal Press couldn't even scratch Zordtch."

"Zordtch?" laughed Valerie.

"He calls his bike Zordtch!" shrieked Donald.

They were both hysterical.

Johnny got up and walked inside. "Get off my property!" he demanded, then slammed the door behind him.

"Well, Don, now what do you want to do?" asked Valerie.

"I don't know, Val, you want to play basketball?" asked Donald.

"All right."

"I guess we shouldn't have said those things to Johnny," said Donald.

"He sure got mad," said Valerie. "I was just trying to get him to not feel so bad about his bottle caps." She kicked at the ground. "I always say the wrong thing. I do it all the time. I hate myself."

"Well, he acts kind of funny sometimes," said Donald. "I've known him longer than you. He'll be all right soon."

Valerie walked with her head down.

Donald tried to cheer her up. "Did you ever notice he looked like a dog?" he asked.

"He looks like my dog!" exclaimed Valerie.

"Really?"

"Exactly!" said Valerie. "I couldn't believe it when I first saw him. I just couldn't believe it."

Donald laughed.

"Except he lacks a tail," said Valerie. "Get it? Johnny Laxatayl. Lacks a tail."

"Johnny lacks a tail," Donald repeated. "Johnny lacks a tail."

"Johnny lacks a tail," said Valerie.

"Johnny lacks a tail," said Donald.

They walked up the street saying it over and over again. "Johnny lacks a tail."

CHAPTER 23

The Beginning of a Long Night

Donald won every game of basketball.

"Well, next time we'll play at my basket," said Valerie.

"What's so special about your basket?" asked Donald.

"No trees," said Valerie.

It was getting close to dinnertime. Donald had to go inside. Valerie walked around to the front.

Johnny was sitting at home in his living room, staring out the window. He wondered what Donald and Valerie were doing. "Well, I don't care," he kept saying to himself. "She's just a girl. Besides, I never liked her anyway."

He put a cigarette in his mouth. "No, what am I doing?" he thought. "I can't smoke in the living room." He put the pack of cigarettes back in his pocket. Then he got a better idea. He walked into the kitchen and threw them away. He stuck them at the bottom of the garbage, inside a cereal box, so that no one would notice them. He never liked them anyway.

Valerie stood out in front of Donald's house and looked down the street toward Johnny's. She didn't want him to be mad at her. She felt bad for having made fun of him and for making fun of his bottle cap collection. "I bet he hates me," she thought. She wanted to go and tell him she was sorry.

She looked back at Donald's house and smiled. She thought Donald was funny. She was glad that they had finally become friends. But *he* didn't look like Popo.

She looked again toward Johnny's house. She wanted to tell him how sorry she was, but she didn't know what to say. It was getting late. She walked home.

Johnny gazed out the living room window. "I never liked her anyway," he said.

CHAPTER 24

Haunted

Johnny got little sleep that night, haunted by what had happened with Valerie and Donald. He put all kinds of horrible thoughts in their heads and imagined bitter arguments with them, then made up his mind never to speak to either of them again.

The next morning his father handed him a list of his responsibilities for the week. He was supposed to clean the garage, wash the car, mow the lawn, vacuum the living room, wash the windows, and shine his shoes, all while balancing a ball on the tip of his nose.

Johnny ripped up the list and told his father to keep his lousy fifty-five cents.

"I'll just have to do the work myself, then," said Harry as he lay down on the couch and thought it over.

Johnny walked out front and kicked the fire hydrant. "Ow," he groaned.

He limped back inside, into the hall closet, and sat down. The closet door shut behind him. There he sat, in the dark, on top of the hatch to the basement.

There was a knock at the door.

"What?" said Johnny.

Christene opened the closet door. "How many cats in a tiger?" she asked.

"Get outta here!" said Johnny. "I'm sick of your idiotic questions!"

Christene's face swelled. "Just 'cause you don't know the answer!" she cried, then slammed the door.

Johnny sat a while longer. Then he stood up, raised the heavy hatch, and stared into the deep, dark hole. He stepped down.

The stairs squeaked. Every step he took echoed throughout the cold, empty basement.

Johnny reached the bottom step and looked out. It seemed as if the bottle caps were there, in the darkness, just as they'd always been. He knew they were gone, that they had been crushed and flattened together by the Metal Press, but in the dark basement it seemed as though they were still there.

A loud bang echoed off the basement walls as the hatch at the top of the stairs slammed shut. Johnny nearly fell over. He felt around for the light switch and flicked it on.

It was empty, so big and empty. He spotted the money on the floor.

Johnny walked across the bald basement floor. What was that smell? Most people wouldn't even recognize it, but there was the faint smell of bottle caps.

He stood over the money. He stared at it, then quickly picked it up and shoved it in his pocket.

There was a flash, then the light went out. Johnny held out his arms and slowly walked until he found the stairs. He stepped up carefully and pushed opened the hatch. He climbed up into the hall closet and walked out into the hall, glad to be out of there. The hatch banged shut behind him.

He saw Christene's socked foot sticking out from under the coffee table and he smiled. "A tiger is a kind of cat," he told her.

Christene pulled in her foot and stuck out her head. "Thank you," she said.

"I'm sorry about what I said to you before," said Johnny. "I didn't mean it."

"I know," said Christene. "You just got rid of some words you didn't want."

Johnny smiled. He liked that.

His father sat up on the couch. "Here, you can still have your fifty-five cents," he said. "We'll forget about responsibility for this week." He paid Johnny his allowance.

"I'll get it done," said Johnny. "Only not right now."

He walked into the kitchen and called Valerie on the telephone. "Let's go spend it," he said.

When she tried to apologize for the things she had said, Johnny told her that she just got rid of some words she didn't want. Then he called Donald.

CHAPTER 25

Junk

In less than a minute after Johnny hung up the telephone, Donald knocked at the front door. He and Johnny waited out front for Valerie.

"That's neat that your parents are letting you spend the money," said Donald.

"It's my money," said Johnny.

"My parents would just make me put it in a bank," said Donald. "Every time I get money, my parents make me put it in the bank."

"I can do anything I want with it," said Johnny. "I have responsibility."

"What are you going to buy?" asked Donald.

Johnny cocked his head. He hadn't thought of that. "I don't know," he answered. "I guess I can buy all sorts of neat stuff."

"Boy, that's so neat!" said Donald. "I'd have to put it in the bank. I never get to buy anything."

Valerie rode up on her bicycle. "Hi, Johnny. Hi, Don," she called.

"Hi, Val," said Donald.

Valerie hopped off of her bike and kicked out the kickstand.

"Come on, Val," said Donald. "You better leave your bike here. We're going to be bringing back a lot of neat stuff."

"Wait a second!" said Valerie. "You just can't go off like that with all that money. We need a plan."

"We got a plan," said Donald. "We're going to buy everything until we run out of money. Come on, Johnny."

"Just hold on!" demanded Valerie. "You don't want to buy a lot of junk, do you? What are you going to do if the first store you come to only sells Flibbets? Are you going to spend all your money on Flibbets?"

"All right, we'll skip that store," said Donald.

"All I want to do is plan ahead," said Valerie. "If we plan ahead we can buy all sorts of really neat stuff. Otherwise, we'll end up with a lot of junk."

"You sound like my parents!" said Donald. "Whenever my grandmother gives me money, my parents make me put it in the bank. They say I have to 'plan for my future.' "

Valerie stood firm.

Donald sighed.

They all sat down on Johnny's front lawn.

"I can see it now," said Donald. "We're not going to buy anything. It's just like when I get money from my grandmother."

"Will you shut up about your grandmother!" said Valerie. "If it was up to you, we'd have eighty-six dollars and thirty-three cents worth of Flibbets!"

"Eighty-six dollars and eighty-eight cents," corrected Johnny. "My father gave me another fifty-five cents."

"Big deal!" said Valerie.

"Okay, Plum," said Donald. "Let's hear your *wonderful* plan."

"All right," said Valerie. "Johnny, go get a pencil and a piece of paper. Make that two pieces."

"Hold on a second!" demanded Donald. "What do you need pencil and paper for?"

"For our budget," replied Valerie.

"A budget!" exclaimed Donald. "A budget? No. No budget. Johnny, are you going to let her make a budget? You're not going to let her make a budget, are you? A budget! Oh man, oh man."

"Listen, Johnny," explained Valerie. "If we make a budget we can figure out exactly what we want to buy. We can figure out exactly how much we should spend on toys, how much on candy, and so on. Then we won't waste any money on junk. We could even buy Duckerman a Flibbet or two."

Donald reared back, ready to slug Valerie, when Johnny announced, "I know what I want to buy!"

"What?" asked Valerie and Donald.

"Cigarettes," answered Johnny. "I want to spend all my money on cigarettes."

Donald and Valerie looked at him aghast.

"I'm not going to smoke them," he went on. "I'm going to bury them. That way nobody else can smoke them."

"Don't be such a dope," said Valerie.

"There will always be more," said Donald. "Maybe Val's right about a budget."

Johnny went inside and returned a minute later with a pencil and two pieces of paper. Valerie took it from him.

"First let's just think of everything we can think of," she said. "I'll write it all down. Then we can go back over it and I'll cross off anything that is only just junk. Then we can budget the rest."

They leaned back on the grass and thought of everything they could think of. After two hours they had covered both sides of both sheets of paper.

"Okay," said Valerie. "I'll read it all back now,

and I'll cross off anything that's junk. Then we'll budget the rest."

Valerie read from the list:

"Baseball cards."

"No," said Johnny. "They're just junk."

Valerie crossed it off. "A toy truck," she read.

"Junk," said Donald.

She crossed it off. "A kite."

"Junk," said Johnny.

"Ping-Pong balls," read Valerie.

"I don't have a Ping-Ping table," said Johnny.

"Junk," they all agreed.

"A model airplane."

"Junk."

"A pogo stick."

"Junk."

"A doll."

"Junk."

"Jaw breakers. Junk. Red hots. Junk. A tool kit. Junk. A camera. Junk. A microscope. Junk. Junk. Junk. Junk. Junk. Junk. Junk. It's all junk!"

After ten minutes they had crossed off everything on the list. It was nothing but junk.

It was a lot harder to spend eighty-six dollars and eighty-eight cents than Johnny had thought. If he only had a quarter or fifty cents, he could go down to the store and buy some junk. But eighty-six dollars and eighty-eight cents was a lot of money. It was too much money to waste on junk.

"Maybe I should put it in the bank," said Johnny, "and wait until something good comes along to buy."

"I knew it!" said Donald. "I knew it! Great plan there, Plum. What a wonderful plan you had. I knew we weren't going to buy anything. It was too good to be true. A budget!"

"It's just a thought," said Johnny.

Donald took a rock out of his pocket and kicked it hard up the street. He walked quickly after it.

"At least we didn't buy any junk!" called Valerie.

"If it was up to you we would have bought nothing but Flibbets!"

"I don't know," said Johnny. "I just don't know what to do."

"Maybe a budget wasn't such a great idea," said Valerie. She got on her bike and rode home.

Johnny walked inside.

CHAPTER 26

It's All Junk

Johnny sat on the edge of the roof with his legs dangling over the side. "It's all junk," he said.

There was a full moon.

"I can't think of anything to buy with my money." he complained. "Everything's junk."

The moon seemed so close that he could almost reach up and touch it.

"Donald and Valerie came over today and we were going to go spend it, but we couldn't think of anything worth buying. It's all junk. It's all just junk.

"I guess I'm really not a little kid anymore. When I was a little kid, there was all kinds of stuff to buy. Now, it's all junk."

The moon hung suspended in orbit. *Listening?*

"I can't ask my parents. They'd tell me to put it in the bank. They'd just tell me to save it for college.

"But I don't know. Maybe I should put it in the bank, just for a little while, just until something comes along that's worth buying.

"But that's the problem! Nothing's ever worth buying. Money can only buy the junk they sell in stores. And that's all they sell in stores—junk.

"The things that are worthwhile can't be bought or sold.

"That's it!" he suddenly exclaimed. He laughed with delight. "I've been worrying over nothing!

"Money can only buy junk." He thought that was wonderful. "The things that are really worth something can't be bought or sold."

The moon was big and round and white and silent.

"Thanks," said Johnny. "I know what I'm going to buy, now." He climbed down from the roof.

CHAPTER 27

All Gone

Early the next morning, Johnny telephoned Donald and Valerie again. "I've got a new plan," he told them.

By seven-thirty they were all out in front of his house.

"We're going to go down to the shopping center," said Johnny, "and we're going to spend all the money."

Donald kicked a rock against the fire hydrant in disgust. "That's the same plan you had yesterday," he said.

"No, it isn't," said Johnny. "Yesterday we wanted to buy neat stuff. Today let's just buy junk!"

"Junk," said Donald. "What a great idea!"

Valerie thought it was the most brilliant plan she had ever heard. She smiled at Johnny. She hadn't known he was so smart.

"Let's go buy some junk!" said Donald.

"Come on," said Johnny.

"We're going to buy some junk," laughed Valerie.

It was a forty-five-minute walk to the shopping center. The first store they came to was one that sold Flibbets.

"It's closed," said Donald. "It doesn't open until nine o'clock."

Johnny looked around. "All the stores are closed," he said.

"Let's go get some breakfast," said Valerie.

"Let's go to Maurecia's!" said Donald. Maurecia's was the best ice-cream parlor in the county. And it was always open, except for February fourteenth when it was closed for the day. February fourteenth was Maurecia's birthday.

"We can get a Purple Bathtub!" said Valerie. A Purple Bathtub was a sundae with twelve different kinds of ice cream and twelve different kinds of toppings, plus bananas, whipped cream, sprinkles, nuts, and cherries.

They ran to Maurecia's. They ordered one Purple Bathtub and three spoons. They were the only ones there. "Oh, and I'd like a glass of prune juice, please," said Valerie, who always had a glass of prune juice with her breakfast.

They looked at each other and laughed. Valerie squeezed Johnny's hand. His toes tingled.

Maurecia brought them their breakfast. It came in a big, purple bowl shaped like an old bathtub.

Three spoons attacked the ice cream. They each tried to get as much as they could. It was a race. Twenty minutes later the bowl was clean and their clothes were a mess.

They leaned back and smiled with delight.

Donald had a spot of ice cream on his chin. And a dab on his nose. And some hot fudge on his fingers. And some caramel syrup in his hair. And some strawberry ice cream in his socks.

"Enough of this good stuff," said Valerie. "Let's go get some junk!"

Johnny paid for the ice cream. Maurecia gave him the bathtub-shaped bowl for a souvenir.

Then they walked back to the shopping center to buy some junk.

First Johnny went into one store and bought a red wagon. "This is to put all the junk in," he explained.

They walked into the Flibbet store and bought three Flibbets.

"We finally sold some!" exclaimed one of the men who worked there. Another man patted him on the back.

Johnny put the Flibbets in the wagon. Donald wheeled it along.

They went into a toy store. They bought some toys and junk and put it in the wagon. Valerie wheeled it along.

They went into a hobby store, leaving the wagon full of junk outside.

"Look, Donald," said Valerie. "They're selling rocks." She showed Donald a box of rocks. The rocks were all brightly colored and had been cut and polished.

"Those are the ugliest rocks I've ever seen," said Donald.

Johnny bought a penny that cost a dollar.

"That's a good deal," said Valerie.

Johnny put the penny in the wagon with the other junk. Then he wheeled the wagon along.

They stopped at a pet store.

Valerie picked out two rubber bones that squealed when you bit them, a green one and a yellow one. "Buy these," she said.

Johnny paid for the bones.

"I got the green one for Popover," Valerie told him.

"What about the yellow one?" asked Johnny.

Valerie laughed. "It's for you," she said as she handed him the rubber bone.

Johnny bit it. It squealed. Then he threw it in the wagon with the other junk.

Donald wheeled it along.

They went into a fancy store that sold fancy junk. Johnny bought a big bottle of perfume for Valerie.

"Yecch!" said Valerie. "This is the worst-smelling junk I've ever smelled." She squirted it at Johnny.

Johnny grabbed her arms and tried to wrestle it away from her. Valerie kept squirting him as long as she could, all over his hair and his face, his arms, his hands, and his clothes.

Finally, Johnny got the bottle away from Valerie and began to squirt her.

Valerie ran.

Johnny ran after her, spraying her back and her hair.

Valerie stumbled and fell and Johnny fell on top of her. He held her down and sprayed it all over her.

"You two stink!" laughed Donald.

Johnny gave the bottle to Valerie and grabbed Donald from behind. He held both of Donald's arms. Valerie poured the rest of the perfume over Donald's head and down his clothes. She threw the empty bottle in the wagon.

They went to some more stores and bought some more junk and then it was time for lunch.

They went back to Maurecia's.

"We'll have another Purple Bathtub," said Johnny.

They finished it in less than fifteen minutes.

"Boy, it's even better for lunch than it is for breakfast!" said Valerie.

Donald wiped his mouth on his sleeve. Then he wiped his sleeve on Valerie's shirt.

Johnny paid for the lunch and Maurecia let them keep the bowl again. Johnny put it in the wagon with the other junk. Then they went to buy some more.

"I ought to buy something for Christene," said Johnny.

"Buy her a baseball bat," said Valerie.

"Christene doesn't know how to play baseball," said Johnny.

"Well, it's time she learned," said Donald.

They went to a sporting goods store and bought a baseball bat and a bunch of balls.

Alongside the shopping center was a little park with some grass, a few trees, two benches, and a lot of birds. A white-haired old gentleman sat on one of the benches and made bird noises. A bird landed on his shoulder.

Donald wandered over in that direction. "Hey Val, Johnny," he called. "Listen."

They walked slowly toward the white-haired gentleman.

"Sh," whispered Valerie, though Johnny and Donald were already walking as quietly as possible.

"Hello," said the old gentleman as they approached. "You kids want to buy a bird tweeter?"

A bird tweeter was a wooden tube with some rings carved in it.

"How much?" asked Johnny.

"How much you got?" asked the old man.

"Don't tell him, Johnny," warned Valerie.

"Okay, then I won't tell you how much they cost," said the old gentleman.

"But then how can we buy any?" asked Donald.

The old man rubbed his chin as he thought it over. "You'll have to guess the price," he decided. "But only one guess."

"You guess, Johnny," said Valerie.

Johnny rubbed his chin. "A dollar, seventy-three," he said.

"No, that's not it," said the old man. "Too bad."

"Give us another chance," said Valerie.

"I said only one guess," the whitehaired gentleman reminded her.

"There are three of us," said Valerie. "We should each get one guess."

"Oh, I suppose that's fair," said the old man. "Go ahead."

"Two dollars and eleven cents," guessed Valerie.

"Nope," said the man.

"Forty-nine cents each, three for a dollar," tried Donald.

The old man's mouth dropped open. "Son of a gun," he muttered.

Johnny paid him a dollar. "I'll take three," he said. "One for me, and one for each of my friends."

"You can't make much money if you make people guess the price," said Valerie.

"If I wanted a lot of money I wouldn't make bird tweeters," the old man replied. He gave Johnny the three tweeters. "I once had a lot of money," he added. "I had a great big house, and a fancy car, and a swimming pool. But now," he patted the park bench, "this is my home."

Valerie sat down on the man's home, next to him.

"Besides," said the gentleman as he winked at Valerie, "you'd be amazed at how many people guess correctly."

"What happened to your house? asked Donald.

"And the car?" asked Johnny.

"And the swimming pool?" asked Valerie.

The man sighed, then answered in a sad, dreamy voice, "I fell in love."

Johnny and Valerie blushed. They looked at each other, then quickly looked away.

"Now, don't get me wrong about love," said the old gentleman. "It was worth it. The house, the car, and the swimming pool, that was just junk."

"That's what we're buying," said Donald. "Junk."

"Except for the bird tweeters. Give me mine, Johnny." said Valerie.

Johnny gave Valerie and Donald each a bird tweeter. They tweeted.

"Well, see ya," said Johnny. "I've still got some money left."

They went into the rest of the stores in the shopping center and bought some more junk.

They had dinner at Maurecia's.

"The usual," said Johnny.

It was even better for dinner than it was for breakfast and lunch. They finished it in less than ten minutes.

Maurecia let them keep the bowl. They had three, one for each of them.

Johnny paid for the ice cream, then left a sixty-two-cent tip.

Outside, he turned his pockets inside out. "All gone," he announced.

Valerie, Donald, and Johnny cheered.

CHAPTER 28

Cluckerman

The three of them headed back to Johnny's house, pulling the wagon full of junk. Along the way, people dropped what they were doing and just watched them pass by. They looked like a walking ice-cream sundae. They smelled like perfume. They sounded like a flock of birds.

Donald kicked a rock as he walked. It was an old grey-and-brown rock, not one of those ugly, colorful, shiny ones that they had seen at the hobby store. The kind of rock that Donald liked couldn't be bought or sold.

As they reached Johnny's house, the Laxatayls came out to greet them.

"What did you buy?" asked Carol.

"Junk," said Johnny, "a wagonful of junk."

"It looks to me like you have some nice things there," said Harry.

"Nope," said Johnny. "It's all just junk."

"Is it good junk?" asked Christene.

"No," said Johnny. "It's only the stuff they sell in stores. Wait. We did get something good." He blew through his bird tweeter.

Valerie and Donald joined in.

At that moment a small boy nervously walked up to

them. It was the same boy who had helped the men from the Metal Press remove the bottle caps. "Here," he said. He held out a bag of bottle caps. "It's not much, but it's a start. I'll bring you a bag every week for the rest of my life. I promise."

"No. That's okay. Keep it," said Johnny. "I'm too old to collect bottle caps anymore. Now I'm collecting junk."

The boy looked at the wagon. "Wow," he said. "Where'd you get all the neat stuff?"

"It's just junk," corrected Donald.

"I don't think so," said the boy. "I think it's neat. You just think it's junk because you have so much. I don't have any toys. I had to sell all my stuff to the Metal Press, even my wagon."

"Do you want this wagon?" asked Johnny.

"Sure!" said the boy. "Can I have it?"

"Sure," said Johnny. He dumped the junk out onto the front lawn. "But there's one condition."

"What?"

"Don't sell it to the Metal Press."

"I won't," the boy promised. He wheeled the wagon away, still not really believing that Johnny had given it to him. It was just like the one he used to have. That's one thing about store-bought stuff—it's all the same. Halfway down the block he turned and yelled, "Thank you!"

Johnny waved back to him.

"Did you get me something?" asked Christene.

"Yep." said Johnny. He reached into the pile of junk on the front lawn and gave Christene the baseball bat.

"Thank you, Johnny," said Christene. "What is it?"

"It's a baseball bat," said Valerie.

"No, that's not a baseball bat," said Christene.

"Yes it is," said Valerie.

"Oh good," said Christene. "I always wanted a baseball bat." She carefully looked it over, then asked, "How does it work?"

"Here give it to me," said Donald. "Pitch me a ball, Val."

Valerie found a ball in the junk and pitched it underhand to Donald. He swung and missed.

"Oh, that looks hard," said Christene. "Let me try."

Valerie pitched it to Christene. She swung and hit the ball on the ground through Valerie's legs.

"Oops, sorry," said Christene.

"What are you sorry about?" asked Valerie. "You hit it. You hit a home run!"

"I thought you were supposed to miss it," said Christene. "Donald missed it."

Donald looked down at the ground in shame. "You're supposed to hit it, Christene," he muttered.

"Oh! That's easy! said Christene. "Pitch me another one, Valerie."

Valerie found another ball and pitched it to Christene. She swung and popped it backward, into the street. It rolled along the gutter and stopped under the tire of a parked car.

"Home run!" yelled Christene.

"I guess I better go home," said Donald. He held his junk under his arm. "Thanks, Johnny. I had a great time. Bye, Val, so long, everybody."

Christene swung her bat against a tree. "Home run!" she called as the leaves fluttered around her.

Donald kicked a rock back up the street toward his house.

"So long, Donald," they all called.

Donald didn't turn around.

"Too bad Donald doesn't live here," said Christene. "Then he wouldn't have to go home."

He kicked the rock home. He felt good. It had been a fun day. It was almost perfect, except when his mother saw him, she told him to take a bath.

He showed her the purple bathtub. "I already took one," he said.

CHAPTER 29

The Return to the Basement

Johnny and Valerie picked up the rest of the junk and carried it inside. They set it down in the hall, next to the closet. "Let's go see it first," said Valerie, "before we bring any of the junk down."

"But there's nothing there," said Johnny.

"I know," said Valerie. "I just haven't seen it since the bottle caps."

Johnny lifted up the hatch inside the closet and they stepped down together. It slammed shut behind them. Valerie raised her eyes. She held onto Johnny's arm. It was dark and they had to step carefully. Johnny liked her holding his arm as he led her down the stairs.

"Careful," said Valerie.

"I've been up and down these stairs a million times," said Johnny. "I know them by heart."

Valerie held on tight.

Back outside, Christene swung her bat against the mailbox, knocking it to the ground. "Home run!" she called.

Valerie looked out across the basement. "Turn on

the light, Johnny," she whispered. "I can't see a thing."

Johnny felt around for the light switch. "It doesn't work," he said. "Oh, I forgot. The bulb blew out." He felt Valerie let go of his arm. "There's nothing to see anyway. It's empty." She took hold of his hand.

"That's what I want to see," said Valerie. "I've never seen it empty."

"Oh, well, then I guess you can see it just as well in the dark as in the light," said Johnny, "since there's nothing to see." He was thinking about Valerie's hand and didn't know what he was saying.

They walked across the basement floor, stopping somewhere in the middle, still holding hands. It was too dark for Johnny to see her, but it felt as if Valerie were looking at him. It made him nervous.

"I can't tell if my eyes are open or shut," said Valerie.

Johnny closed and opened his eyes. She was right.

Valerie changed her grip on his hand so that their fingers interlocked. "You have ice cream on your fingers," she said.

Johnny held his breath, cautiously reached over, and took hold of Valerie's other hand so that they stood facing each other. "So do you," he said.

"Well I do now, anyway," said Valerie. She squeezed his hands.

Johnny couldn't see her but he thought she looked beautiful.

Above there was a loud *crash* as Christene smashed a glass vase. "Home run!" she called.

"Don't do that, Princess." said her father.

Johnny's eyes slowly began to adjust to the darkness. He could see Valerie smiling at him. He squeezed her hands.

"Hi," whispered Valerie.

He wanted to kiss her. He thought it was the dumbest thing he'd ever wanted to do, yet that was what he wanted to do.

But how? He couldn't ask her. What could he say, "Do you want to kiss?" He couldn't say that! It sounded so stupid.

Valerie started to say something, then just sighed.

"Johnny, come get your junk out of the hall!"

He wondered how long this could last. How long could they stand there, holding hands and looking at each other? He could see her pretty well now. It's easier to look at someone when you can't see them. How long had they been standing there already? He had no idea. He just wanted to kiss her. If only it wasn't such a dumb thing to want to do.

Crash!

"Home run!"

"Give me the bat, Princess. Give Daddy the bat like a good little girl."

Valerie smiled. She squeezed his hands.

"John-ny!"

Johnny sighed. If he wanted to play checkers, that would be easy. He could say, "Hey Valerie, do you want to play checkers?" But he didn't want to play checkers. He wanted to kiss her.

Valerie smiled. Her eyes seemed to sparkle.

A strange thought occurred to him. Could it be that she had been thinking the same thing, that she wanted to kiss him too, only she was afraid to say it? Sure, it sounded crazy, but maybe it was true.

Valerie started to say something, then looked away.

Was *that* what she was going to say?

"What?" Johnny whispered.

Valerie blushed. "Nothing."

"Oh," said Johnny.

"What?" asked Valerie.

"I said oh," said Johnny.

"Oh," said Valerie.

"What?" asked Johnny.

Valerie laughed.

Johnny took a deep breath.

"John-ny! Johnny, where are you?"

Valerie leaned a bit toward him. They kissed.

"He's in the basement," said Christene, "with Valerie."

JOIN IN THE ADVENTURES WITH BUNNICULA AND HIS PALS
by James Howe

HOWLIDAY INN

69294-5/ $4.99 US/ $6.50 Can

THE CELERY STALKS AT MIDNIGHT

69054-3/ $4.50 US/ $5.99 Can

RETURN TO HOWLIDAY INN

71972-X/ $4.50 US/ $5.99 Can

DEW DROP DEAD

71301-2/ $4.50 US/ $5.99 Can